The
Last Stage from Opal

The
Last Stage from Opal

KELLY P. GAST

DOUBLEDAY & COMPANY, INC.

GARDEN CITY, NEW YORK

1978

All of the characters in this book
are fictitious, and any resemblance to
actual persons, living or dead,
is purely coincidental.

ISBN: 0-385-13473-8
Library of Congress Catalog Card Number: 77-26525
Copyright © 1978 by Doubleday & Company, Inc.
All Rights Reserved
Printed in the United States of America
First Edition

The
Last Stage from Opal

CHAPTER I

Wes stood before his tent chopping up a dead tamarack. It was about the last wood he was going to find on this flat and he knew he would have to stir his stumps and somehow gain access to a horse and wagon before fall. But that was months away, and if he were to last out a winter here, he had to worry about putting up a cabin before then. There were other problems too, like a well and a garden. But most of all, there was the problem of money.

He tried not to think about it as he reveled in the simple joy of swinging an ax in the morning sun, watching pitchy wood split into neat billets. There was still a lot of stiffness in his lanky body. Some, he supposed, was going to be permanent. The sun came a few minutes higher over the eastern range, and he peeled his flannel shirt over his head while wishing some enterprising seamstress would simplify this maneuver by learning to run that opening all the way down like they did in the Orient.

The woodpile had grown to a respectable size, and he was just beginning to consider if it might not be time to seduce a tin stove into producing coffee and flapjacks when he heard the distant rattling echo of a .44. Before he had time to wonder why anybody would waste revolver ammunition on a jackrabbit, the hunter apparently changed his mind and fired a rifle. That bellowing Sharps, Wes knew, wouldn't leave the shredded ears of a rabbit. He also knew that this time of year there was nothing else worth hunting.

Some of those muckers up at the mine feeling their oats and wasting their pay, he decided.

A quarter mile away the barely visible tracks of the Opal road disappeared into the foothills that turned sundown into a midafternoon proposition in this country. At times when the wind was right, he could actually feel, if not hear, the sudden pressure change that came whenever the Opal mine lit off a shot.

Which had nothing to do with the way his tin stove was laying down on the job. He knelt awkwardly, his right leg sticking straight out, and blew until the tamarack abruptly burst into bright yellow flames. A hundred yards behind the tent he had dug a yard deeper into a sinkhole and curbed his efforts with two bottomless Sears Roebuck cracker boxes until, by taking infinite pains, he could draw a bucket of clear water. He put some to boil for coffee and, with another glance at a day too good to waste in cooking, decided to make do with oatmeal instead of flapjacks.

Dead tamarack roared with the enthusiasm of a young forest fire and soon both pots were boiling. He sifted oats into bubbling water under the watchful eye of a whiskey jack perched on the ridgepole of his tent. The jay ceased its chatter for a moment and he heard the distant clink and creak of harness. He glanced up and saw the weekly stage from Opal.

It would pass within a hundred yards of his tent. He supposed he ought to go through the motions and offer the driver coffee and his horses water. Not that Wes was that fond of having his water hole all muddied up, but a man had to preserve the decencies, no matter what he might think of his neighbors.

Anyhow, Wes told himself, the ancient who drove the weekly stage from the county seat to Opal had never done him dirt. He was rummaging through his portable kitchen to see if he had any condensed cream when he heard the outraged shriek of the whiskey jack who flapped, raking its bill in the dust in frantic efforts to rid itself of a gob of boiling-hot oatmeal. The camp robber flew away with a final burst of profanity and Wes looked toward the foothills again. Stage should have been here by now.

It wasn't. Halfway from the spot where it had exited the foothills, the four-horse team dawdled to crop at sparse spring grass. Old blowhard must be drunk again, Wes decided. He didn't have any canned milk. Didn't have any butter either.

He sprinkled lumpy brown sugar over his oatmeal and wolfed it down with heavily sugared black coffee. He was washing cup and bowl in the half-round Scotch bowl that was his dishpan, pot, skillet, oven, and on occasion his gold pan when he realized the stage had not moved a hundred yards in the last fifteen minutes. Even making allowances for some drunken, time-served miner with enough residual delicacy not to nasty seat cushions, this was too long.

Something was wrong. Wes tried to tell himself it was none of his affair, but he knew that, like it or not, it was liable to turn into his business. It was too close and he was the only man around. Only stranger too, he realized.

He wished for his field glasses but, like several other things that had long been a part of him, these too were gone. He squinted at the stage and couldn't see anyone. He sighed and began walking up the barely visible track that was the road to Opal.

Wes Brooks was a fraction over six feet and had done a lot of walking in his life. But that had been before he had been forced to learn how to do it without his right kneecap. In the last few months he had practiced various modes and found that he seemed to last longest and limp least with a slight rolling swing that took his stiff knee in an outward arc to miss the ground on the forward stroke. He had experimented with various makeshifts and finally surrendered to the inevitable that he was, for the rest of his natural life, going to wear one boot out twice as fast as the other.

He stumped along, reminding himself that the sun was out, that it was springtime, that he was really not all that old, that the world was full of more deserving men with far worse luck than his.

Still the four horses grazed, dragging the stagecoach willy-nilly behind them. There was nobody on the box, and as he came closer, Wes saw there were no passengers inside either. Abruptly he remembered the shots. A rifle had replied to a revolver. He came closer and the reins were not tied to the brake pole.

The lead horse gave him a look of equine unconcern and pulled ahead for another clump of bunch grass. Wes caught a check rein and worked his way carefully alongside four unknown quantities until he could capture the handful of reins that draped over the doubletree. He studied the box and tried to find some easy way of mounting. With a stiff knee there was no easy way. He tossed the reins over the brake pole and began pulling himself up hand over hand. There was blood on the seat. The strongbox was gone.

Wes was suddenly acutely aware of his position. He didn't possess so much as a slingshot. Ought to take those reins and gallop nonstop back to the county seat and sheriff, he guessed. But somewhere a mile back up in the foothills the driver might be gasping his life out.

In Wes's line of work he hadn't had that much to do with horses. A whip lay on the box. He would never have enough hands to use it. He coiled it around his waist as he had seen drovers do and addressed himself to the fistful of reins. Eight of the damned things!

He sighed and wondered if he would end up spilling the

coach—end up with another stiff leg. Sighing again, he began taking up the slack one by one and figuring out which rein led where. Finally he had all the lefts in one hand, the rights in the other. He kicked the brake pole free of its ratchet and tried to even up tension. With a silent prayer for the coachwork, he rattled the reins and clucked.

The horses acted just as if he knew what he was doing. Their heads dropped below the hames and they began pulling. He swung the coach in a hundred-yard circle through scant sage and bunch grass and a moment later the team settled down at a fast trot heading back up toward Opal. It was a mile before he came to the body in the road.

Stopping a four-horse team was a little more complicated than starting it, but finally he got the idea through the off-wheel horse's head too, albeit with considerable punishment to three blameless mouths. There had to be some quick way of tugging on just one set of reins. But how? Anyway, they were finally stopped. He set the brake, hitched reins around it, and swung down, lowering himself with both hands.

The old man had a bloody spot in the middle of his back. When Wes rolled him over there was a half-inch hole in the front of his flannel shirt. The stage driver's eyes were wide open and covered with dust.

Wes struggled until he had managed to horse the body into the passenger portion of the stage. He threw a lap robe over the old man's face. He gave the ground a cursory study for footprints and hoofprints, but there was nothing readable. Nor was there any sign of a weapon. He studied the site for another moment trying to decide whether the ground was too hard or if somebody had taken the time to wipe out any tracks. There was only a single clear impression of something three cornered. After a second he knew it had to be where a corner of the strongbox had punctured the flinty earth.

A tracker or a Pinkerton might make something more out of it. Wes was neither. He unfastened the reins from the brake and sorted them out again. There had to be an easier way to do this. Maybe if he were to knot them into two groups . . . but every time the coach went up a rise or down a gully, he had to adjust the fistful of reins that passed through hames loops and bellyband rings and an infinitude of nameless eyelets from lead horse to wheel horse and finally to his hands.

It was six of one and half a dozen of the other whether he drove downhill toward the river and county seat and what passed for civilization—or drove the slightly shorter distance uphill back to the mine. But down at the county seat he could waste hours or even days in pointless explanations. He decided to take the stage back up to the mine and let them decide. After all, it had been their strongbox.

Opal lay in a cañon at the foot of a tailings dump, its single street divided by a creek whose pollution was brown foamed and total. Wes urged the stage up the street, looking for the depot. It was his first visit to the mining town in spite of having staked out on the flat just after the thaw. He admired the Chinese laundry and restaurant. He supposed the Celestials in this country might have had time to master not just the appearance but possibly even the taste of American grub. There was a profusion of saloons and he pondered the wisdom of a company town that encouraged drunkenness.

But if the company were to discourage them, saloons would merely multiply beyond the fringes of the town and siphon off money from the closed circuit economy of a company town. He wondered where the stage depot was, but mostly he wondered if he would ever be able to stop these suddenly spirited, almost galloping horses if ever he were to find it. Then abruptly the horses slowed and began turning. They knew the town better than he did.

A few hundred yards above him, near the headframe, a whistle shrilled so piercingly that Wes nearly dropped the reins. The horses were still moving briskly and he was wondering if he could persuade them to stop without making a fool of himself in front of all these gawkers when abruptly the stage passed through a false-fronted gateway into a corral large enough to turn a four-horse team. Without any effort on his part the horses halted.

A short, balding man in a green eyeshade emerged from an office breathing hard and apparently building up a head of steam. He stopped abruptly when he saw Wes. "Who're you?"

"Name's Wes Brooks. Live about halfway to the county seat."

"Where's Gabriel?"

"If Gabriel's the driver, that's probably him inside." Wes gestured at the passenger compartment.

By now gawkers were congregating to learn why the once-a-week stage had not continued on its appointed rounds. Wes began lowering himself to the ground, and halfway down the whip around his waist snagged and loosened until the leaded handle thumped his knee. He stood stretching awkwardly and wrapping the whip again while several of the gawkers got the stiffening body of the driver out of the stage and carried it into the office.

"Where's the strongbox?" the agent demanded.

Wes gave the short man a pitying look and shook his head. "You got any law around here?" he asked.

The stage agent looked around, then pointed at a puffy, red-faced man in calfskin vest and slightly undersized derby who strode through the false-front archway. "There's the marshal."

The pudgy man elbowed his way through the crowd and

faced up to Wes. "Saw you come drivin' in," he said. "What happened?"

Wes told him what little he knew.

The company bull looked at the station agent. "There goes my job," he muttered.

"*Your* job!" the little man snapped.

Wes was wondering what either of them could have done to prevent it when the bull turned to glare at him from piggy eyes. "Only two shots?"

Wes nodded.

"And you say it was a forty-four and a Sharps?"

Wes nodded again.

"How do you know?"

"I know."

"Just who the hell are you anyhow?"

"I'm a law-abidin' citizen who's wasted enough time tending to somebody else's business."

The pudgy man reddened. He took a deep breath and held it a moment. "No need to git huffy," he said, "but it'd help if you had a name."

"Wester Brooks," Wes said stiffly.

"Old Gabe alluz carried a Sharps," the green-eyeshaded man offered.

"That's real helpful," the town bull said acidly. "All we gotta do now is find the only man in the West carries a forty-four."

"And has a Sharps and a strongbox full of silver bullion," Green Eyeshade added, oblivious of the company bull's irony.

"That's about the size of it," Wes agreed. "And I've just done my good deed for the day. If you'll excuse me now." He turned to leave.

"Just a minute!"

Wes turned once more to the pudgy man. "Yes?"

But Green Eyeshade and the bull were looking at the whip still coiled round his waist. Wes began unwinding it. "Uh—you drove the stage back here, didn't you?" Green Eyeshade asked.

"Kind of looks like it." Abruptly Wes realized that the horses' habit of turning into this corral had made it look to all these strangers as if he knew how to drive a four-in-hand. He continued uncoiling the whip.

Suddenly the bull was pleading. "Look," he said, "we're shorthanded and there ain't that many men left any more as knows how to drive four horses. Would you mind takin' the stage back down to the county seat?"

Before Wes could refuse the green-eyeshaded agent added, "Pay you five dollars."

It was an offer Wes could not refuse.

"Give us an hour to write some letters," the company bull added. "You might's well go over to Yee Wing's and have a bite to eat."

It sounded like an excellent idea, but Wes didn't have the money and he was damned if he was going to weaken his bargaining power by admitting it. "See you later," he said, and stepped out of the office.

Opal's single street had been nearly deserted when he drove into town. Now it thronged with hard-looking, dirty men heading for the nearest saloon. He remembered the whistle. Shift change, he supposed. He wondered idly how much silver the mine had lost in that strongbox.

Not that he really gave a damn. If the management were like most mines', they could pay their muckers twice as much, could install modern, safe machinery, and still make an obscene profit for some easterner who would roll good cigars and better whiskey around his mouth while explaining that miners were just a lot of scum who would only drink it all up and could not be trusted to appreciate the finer things in life.

The whip's shot-loaded butt was banging his hip with each step as heavily as if he still wore a pistol. Should have left the damned thing back on the stage. He strolled slowly so's not to limp until he stood just down the street from the false-fronted stage depot—which put him directly across the street from the Chinese restaurant.

It had been a while since his hasty breakfast of oatmeal, but he could wait until he was back at his own diggings to eat again. Had to, whether he wanted to or not. But one thing for damned sure: He was going to get his five dollars at this end of the line and not depend on any promises at the other end. With five dollars he could lay in some bacon and coffee and flour and maybe pick up some kind of a gun that would make life shorter for the rabbits and easier for him.

Somebody jostled him and Wes started from his reverie. A half dozen glowering men surrounded him. One of them carried a pick handle. "Why'd you kill old Gabe?" he demanded.

CHAPTER II

It was odd—as if his mind were divided into two watertight compartments. Half of Wes was struggling with a mixture of annoyance, outrage, and just plain fear at this unexpected menace. But even as he struggled to remind himself that he was no longer a whole man, that he was not so nimble as once, he was already reacting.

With his left leg, he stepped forward toward the man with the pick handle, moving his arm back to take full advantage of forward momentum. His fist landed squarely on the nose of the man who had accused him. Pick Handle's nose blossomed into a red fountain as his weapon fell from nerveless hands and clattered hollowly on the wooden sidewalk.

Now he was for it, Wes realized as he surveyed the ring of miners who stood in a half circle pinning him against the building front. But his body was already doing the right thing. He swung his stiff leg behind him like some bowing eighteenth-century courtier as he picked up the pick handle. He brought its heavy end down smartly on the toe of the bloody-nosed man's boot.

Still not quite realizing what had happened to their champion, the half-dozen men goggled. Wes studied them a moment, then tried once more to get the bloody-nosed man's attention by rapping on his toes with the pick handle. "Proper form when addressing a stranger," he explained icily, "is, 'Why did you kill old Gabe, *sir?*'"

"We was just a funnin'," one of the miners mumbled.

"Funnin' *what?*" Wes hefted the pick handle.

"Funnin', *sir,*" the other hastened.

"Any further questions?" Wes snapped.

It seemed that there were none.

"Then fall out and carry on." Wes stood erect, pick handle tucked under his arm, and watched them scurry off down the street. At the corner the bloody-nosed man hesitated long enough to look back at him. It was the confused look of a horned animal struggling to understand how a carefree afternoon of people-tossing had turned into a sword sliding past a collarbone.

Wes stood rigid for some time, knowing that if he were to move he would betray himself. Finally his body would obey him and he continued his stroll up the single street that was Opal. Damn! He was going to have to learn not to react that way. This time he had emerged unscathed. He had to remember that knee, remember that he was not the man he used to be—nor in the position he used to be.

Moving with a step carefully measured to minimize his limp, he strode past a Chinese café, a Chinese laundry, and a block later, he was at the edge of Opal's high-rent district. Ahead lay only a handful of shacks, some of which must have been built before the town came into existence, since they faced the single street from casual angles.

There was a tiny footbridge across the foam-flecked creek that split Opal's single street. He crossed it, suddenly feeling eyes upon his back. A woman was studying him from the doorway of one of the shacks. She smiled and beckoned. Wes waved back, hoping for her sake that later in the afternoon she would get herself together and present a more attractive package.

Back uphill miners still poured in and out of saloons. Wes wondered if he had been forgotten already. Fat chance, he decided. Any blowhard stupid enough to accost a stranger with a question like that would probably devote his life to nursing a grudge, convincing himself that it had been an unprovoked attack, that the community would not know a moment's peace until Wes had been lynched.

It had been a stupid thing to do. Wes knew he should have turned it into a joke, jollied them out of it. But it was too late now. Now he would have to live with it. Or die with it. . . . He breathed deeply and faced the problem of how to walk a couple of hundred yards back to the stage depot—uphill yards, without limping too obviously.

Up there among the miners, a slim figure was threading its way with ballet grace through them, heading downhill toward him. As the pirouetting, slightly pigeon-toed youngster came closer, Wes could distinguish black braids.

"Mr. Brooks?" the Indian boy asked.

Wes nodded.

"They're waiting for you up at the stage depot."

Surely an hour had not passed already. Green Eyeshade and the company bull, he decided, must both be fast men with a pen.

He moved at what he supposed must seem a leisurely pace to anyone else, even though it was all Wes could do without exaggerating his limp. Beside him, the Indian boy walked, studying him with an attitude that was neither covert nor stoic. "Did you really thump Hoggins?" the boy finally asked.

Wes sighed. The streets were full of miners washing rock dust from their throats, but the town was not that big. He wondered if there was a single person on the streets of Opal who had not gotten one version or another of the story by now.

"Now, whatever gave you an idea like that?" he asked.

But the boy was looking at his waist. After a moment he

looked up. "They say it was a stranger with a whip and he didn't even use it."

Wes sighed again. He was so used to the weight of a pistol that he had totally forgotten the shot-loaded whip butt thumping his thigh with each step. He searched for something to say and concluded there was nothing worth adding to the subject. "Who's Hoggins?" he finally asked.

"He's the man usually carries that pick handle you got under your arm."

Wes wondered why he was still carrying the damned thing. He tossed it into the brown-foamed creek and watched it bob downstream toward wherever all this hopelessly poisoned water ended up. Then he turned and stumped uphill toward the stage depot again. They walked along in a companionable silence, threading their way through roistering miners who, he abruptly noticed, were more than usually careful to stay out of his way. "Who's Hoggins?" he repeated.

The Indian boy gave him an odd look. "Got to be careful what I say," he muttered.

"Why?"

The boy looked at him again and hesitated a moment. "'Cause I'm an Indian—that's why!" he blazed.

"Oh. One of those towns," Wes mused.

"Is there another kind?"

"Don't rightly know," Wes admitted. "I been out of the country for a while."

"If he was an Indian," the boy said, "they'd call Mr. Hoggins a bad Injun and they'd give him a fair trial and then they'd hang him."

Wes studied the boy with renewed interest. Clad in flannel shirt and worn Levis, the boy still clung to moccasins and braids. His face was broad and coppery, of a brighter hue than Wes was used to seeing. "You from around here?" he asked.

The boy nodded and they turned into the tricked-out false arch that marked the entry into the stage company's yard. Green Eyeshade and the puffy-faced company bull in the too-small derby hat were waiting. "Ready to go?" Green Eyeshade asked.

"Not quite."

"What else do you need?"

"No tickee, no washee."

While Green Eyeshade muttered and rushed into the office the puffy-faced company bull handed Wes a fistful of unstamped, hastily scribbled letters. One, Wes noted, was for the sheriff of Okapogum County whose name seemed to be Hurley.

The stage agent came out of the office again with a small gold coin and a receipt for five dollars that Wes dutifully signed. He stuck the letters in a pocket and climbed once more onto the box of the stage. "Anybody inside?" he asked. It seemed that there was not.

Wes had been devoting some thought to how he would grip the reins. He untied them, got his stiff leg comfortable while sorting out the reins, and breathed a silent prayer that the horses would know more than he and would not be so inurbane as to expose his ignorance for all these Philistines to see. Finally he guessed he had the reins right. He gripped them firmly and clucked.

Nothing happened.

He clucked again and still the four horses stood easy. Wes took a deep breath, gave a shrill yell and slapped reins on their backs. The stage lurched forward and tore through the arch into the street where it swung wide. Startled miners scampered out of the way. Praying he would not run over somebody, Wes gripped the reins and tried to act as if the stage were not driving him. From the corner of his eye he saw the Indian boy's hero-worshiping gaze. He wondered if he was fooling everybody. Surely there must still be men in these western states who could remember how to drive four-in-hand.

Five dollars . . . He had the coin secure in the depths of a pocket he had tested for leaks. With five dollars he could lay in a few things, pick up some kind of a weapon, get himself prepared for the struggle to come if he were to survive until winter—providing he could just get this stage down to the county seat without wrecking it.

The horses moved down Opal's single street, unable to decide whether to trot or gallop. By now the thronging miners had thinned out and he made it out of town without accident. At one of the odd-angled shacks a woman beckoned and he wondered if he ought to stop for passengers. Then he realized it was the same woman who had greeted him when he was on foot. Persistent . . . but this time she had combed her hair and looked a little better.

Out of town and on more level ground the four-horse team settled down to a trot. Wes clung to the reins and experimented with various methods of adjusting tension as team and coach undulated over the gently rolling flat. Maybe if he were to grip the wheel horse reins between ring and little fingers . . .

It was early afternoon now and he realized he was going to have to finish the run after dark. Should have waited till next day, he guessed. But the company bull and Green Eyeshade must have their own excellent reasons for wanting the news to get to the county seat as rapidly as possible.

It was funny. In the press of events Wes had practically forgotten the holdup. He hadn't even thought to ask how much had been lost. He sighed. Chances were the information would all be there in the letters for the sheriff and others in the county seat.

He passed the spot where he had picked up the dead driver's body. At least he thought that was the place. With the sun high in the afternoon sky, everything was different. The horses showed signs of wanting to stop. They were, he supposed, as much creatures of habit as are men. Having stopped here once, they would assume it was part of the daily routine. He yelled and slapped reins until they were trotting once more. A half hour later he saw the ridgepole of his tent. The camp robber had returned to roost on it. He tried to remember if he had left anything edible outside. Damn, was he ever hungry!

It took less effort than he had expected to get the tiring horses to come to a halt. He tied the reins to the brake pole and lowered himself awkwardly to the ground. The whiskey jack watched with a proprietary interest as he whittled shavings and started a fire in the tin stove. While it was heating up he mixed flour, salt, water, and baking powder for bannock and greased the skillet.

While it was baking he tried to decide what he needed the most. More flour, corn meal, beans, and grease, he decided. If he could just find a cheap weapon somewhere, there had to be meat of some kind around here—even if he had to hike up into the hills to get it.

From his place the next couple of miles toward the county seat were level and straight. He had decided against wasting time on coffee, so he drove with one hand while munching on steaming bannock with the other. The worst thing about this diet was not the inevitable scurvy; it was the insidiously habit-forming nature of a monotonous diet that did not leave one with any desire or hunger for anything else. He was going to have to force himself to hunt up some fruit or vegetables soon if he wanted to keep his teeth.

It was still daylight when he reached the edge of the flat and began the hairpin, hair-raising descent down to the next level of this stepped country. The horses began their fluttery, nervous descent, kicking and whinnying as the coach pushed them downhill. He sawed on the reins, struggling to control their desire to outrun the coach, and finally gave up, transferring reins to one hand and dedicating his other hand and his good foot to the brake pole. Finally the breeching straps stopped cutting into the horses' rumps and they descended the narrow, hairpin road at a less harrowing pace. The coach's back wheels were locked and skidding. How many trips, he wondered, did this company expect to get before the steel tires wore thin or loosened and fell off?

The coach rounded the final switchback and they were on level ground again. He let off the brake and held the reins loosely until the horses had galloped out their nervousness. A mile later they had once more settled down to a trot.

Then they slowed to a cautious walk as the trail abruptly changed from dust to firm ground, then mud. Moments later the stage was axle deep in a creek. Wes studied the sparkling water and wondered if this was the same brown foam that had flowed down Opal's single street. Water was supposed to purify and regenerate itself by flowing only sixty feet over gravel. Wes was as inclined to believe this as he had been a fisherman's story about lobsters growing new claws. Somehow, neither sounded very probable.

"Jes' hold it right there, stranger," a voice called. "Keep yore hands in plain sight right on the reins."

Wes sighed. He hauled at the reins until the horses halted, barely on solid ground. The coach's back wheels were still in nearly a foot of water. "If you're out to rob the stage you're too late," he said. "Somebody beat you to it this morning."

"Dew tell. Now jes' toss down yore gun."

"I'm afraid you're several months late for that," Wes said. "If you're interested in the horses or the stage, just tell me which way to walk and you're welcome."

"Jes' come down off the left-hand side of that box and walk straight ahead where I can get a look at you, young feller."

It was both pointless and dangerous to try to do anything else, Wes decided. He tied the reins around the brake pole and lowered himself carefully. The front end of the stage was still in a couple of inches of water too, and as he came down, he felt it penetrate his worn boots. Something else in his life that was going to require serious thought—if he could just get this stage delivered to the county seat. "Where are you?" he asked as he walked up to stand beside the lead horse.

"Don't make no never mind," the voice said, but at that moment he saw the grizzled ancient with what he would be willing to swear was a .50-caliber Hawken rifle. Clad in greasy buckskins and with white hair down over his ears, the old man was totally incongruous in this short-haired era.

But, venerable or not, the rifle he pointed at Wes was real. Nor did Wes have the slightest doubt about it being loaded. He wondered if the old man was totally sane. Did he think this was still the wild West, that people could get away with robbing stages in nineteen-oh-two? Then Wes reminded himself that this stage had already been robbed once today, that one driver had already died.

"Where's old Gabe?" the grizzled man asked.

That again? Wes made a lightning decision that honesty was probably the best policy. "Dead," he said. "Killed by the last drygulcher pointed a rifle at this stage."

Apparently it was the right answer because after a moment of shocked silence the rifle barrel pointed away from him. "Dead?" the old man echoed. "Then who're you?"

Wes resisted the temptation to say he was the guy who put the vice in advice. "I found him shot," he explained. "People up in Opal paid me to drive the stage down to the county seat."

By now the butt of the Hawken was resting on the ground. The grizzled ancient bent stiffly to let off the cock, then cupped his hands over the muzzle as he studied Wes. "Soldier, ain't you?"

"Nope," Wes said. "Country don't ever seem to run out of wars but ever so often they run out of money to fight them."

The old man stared quizzically for a moment at Wes. "Stranger here, ain't ye?"

Wes allowed this was a fair guess.

"Don't know anybody in these parts?"

Wes didn't. Since he had gotten off the riverboat he had been totally devoted to grabbing a piece of land and getting set for the winter. Even if he were inclined toward gregariousness, Wes had had enough experiences of late to cure him of this habit.

Still, the old man was studying him. Wes wondered if he ought to take the old man's gun away from him. He decided against it. The old geezer was no longer threatening him and it was a bit late to teach new tricks to any dog as old as this one.

Just as he had decided against disarming the old man, the buckskin-clad stranger turned his back on Wes. He strode into the stream and inspected the interior of the empty stage. Wes knew it was empty. He wondered what the oldster found so amusing about this fact.

He was still wondering when the white-haired man turned once more to face him. "Yo're gonna git a royal welcome in Okapogum. I can jes' see that."

Wes wondered what was so funny about it.

CHAPTER III

He was still wondering when, an hour later with his feet still squishy in his worn boots, he watched the sun go down. How much farther to Okapogum? He was tempted to camp for the night, but he and the horses would both be hungrier and thirstier by morning and he didn't know how many other oddly inclined strangers might show up to spoil a man's sleep. He rattled the reins and encouraged the tired horses. As far as he could remember the country from his single trip out to his diggings, it was mostly level from here on in—except for the final five-hundred-foot scramble down to the level of the river.

The stage rocked along as the horses picked their way through the gathering darkness, following a road they knew better than Wes did. Gradually, he was beginning to understand some of the messages the four horses were sending back to him via the reins.

He remembered his boyhood, before life had taken him in a direction few horses went, when an aged man from a neighboring farm had explained the secret of managing horses: "You got to have at least as much sense as the horse," old Stanton had said. Now why was he remembering that fount of rural wisdom after all these years? Because old Stanton, probably twenty years dead by now, was very like the buckskin-clad ancient who had stopped him at the ford. And he hadn't even gotten the name of this grizzled ancient with the Hawken rifle.

He glanced wistfully at the sky, but there was neither sign nor promise of a moon. He could smell the river now—a heavy, sour smell of poplar and willow that overlay the faint scent of blooming sage. Sniffing, he caught a light stink of coal smoke. There were no railroads here in this valley, nor did the steamboats, whose travel was limited to the few months of high water, burn anything but wood. A smelter? He could not recall having seen one as he had come through this country on his way in.

What difference did it make? He squinted into the darkness, praying the horses would not let him down. How much farther was it to Okapogum?

An hour passed and abruptly the country in front of him was even blacker than black. He almost whipped up the horses when abruptly he realized they probably knew something he didn't. They halted and stood tiredly. Wes tied reins to the brake pole and lowered himself stiffly to the ground. He walked to the lead team and stood staring into darkness. There was no ground in front of them. He squinted and sniffed. Somewhere ahead—and five hundred feet below them lay the county seat. The horses were afraid to tackle the downgrade in the dark. So was Wes. He unfastened their bits from one side, so the unfortunate beasts could rest their mouths. No doubt a teamster would have unharnessed and hobbled them, but even in daylight—even knowing where the hobbles were, if there were any, Wes wasn't sure of his ability to unharness them. He knew damned well that unless he were to take the harness off in daylight, he would never discover how to get it back on them in the morning. "Sorry," he murmured, and curled up in the back of the stage to wait for dawn.

When he awoke it was dawn. But it was not dawn that had awakened him. A man was shaking him.

For the first time in his life Wes felt old. He had known

he would never be the man he was but . . . Instantly he was awake. He reached reflexively for something that was no longer there. The movement was not lost by the red-mustached man who shook him. "Think I'd be this close to a stranger if he was heeled?" he asked with a hint of amusement.

"Who're you?" Wes asked.

"I was about to ask the same question," Red Mustache said. "And the whole town's wonderin' why the stage spent the night up here in plain sight instead of comin' into town." Wes's eyes came into bleary focus and he saw the tin star for the first time. "Would your name be Hurley?" he asked.

The sheriff nodded, standing far enough away to keep his gun hand free.

"Got a letter for you in my pocket," Wes said. "If you don't object to my moving mighty slow and careful, I'll hand it to you."

"Slow and careful makes for a long and happy life in this country," the sheriff agreed.

Wes fished the handful of letters from his pocket and found the one for the sheriff. He put it in the open doorway of the coach and moved back while the sheriff picked it up. Hurley gave him another cautious glance before opening the letter. "Whatcher name?" he asked when he finished reading the company bull's report.

Wes told him.

"Wes Brooks . . ." Hurley chewed the name over thoughtfully. "Swear I'd heard that name somewhere," he mused.

Wes shrugged.

"Well," the sheriff mused, "I guess you'll do until another report comes in."

Wes wasn't sure what he meant. Nor was he sure he cared to know.

"Never drove this run before?"

Wes shook his head.

"Don't trust the brake," the sheriff advised. "I'll see you down in town."

Wes wanted to ask what alternatives there were to an untrustworthy brake, but already the sheriff had decided he was harmless and was gone. Wes got out of the stage and stretched. It was a cool, clear morning and the sun was already up. He yawned and wished he had coffee. The horses gazed at him in mute supplication. He stared back guiltily, wishing he'd had enough knowledge of harness to dare unhitch them last night.

But he hadn't, so that was that. He shrugged and studied the precipice ahead. It was nearly vertical, a faint switchback more like a bobsled run than a road winding down the five-hundred-foot drop-off from one flat to the next. Directly below him lay the thirty-odd houses and buildings that composed the county seat.

How was he going to get a stage down this incline without spooking the horses? He looked at them for advice. If they knew how, they weren't saying.

Hurley had warned him not to trust the brake. But damn it, the stage had been making this run once a week for—he didn't know how long. Longer than he had been in the country. He considered the dusty track around him. Had his predecessor hidden anything in the way of a drag around here, perhaps something heavy that was carried only up and down this hill instead of the whole distance to Opal? A thorough search of the area took less than a minute in this barren country of sagebrush and scant bunch grass. There was no drag.

He opened the boot, but there was nothing of any use to him inside that leather-covered luggage rack. Which left nothing apart from the passenger compartment. He went back in where he had slept and considered. There was room for a very shallow storage compartment—possibly—beneath the seat cushions. He picked up the front cushion and sure enough, there was a compartment there. A practically forgotten compartment, he guessed, for the board beneath the cushion was wedged so solidly that he managed to open it only with the corkscrew that was part of his jackknife. Finally the board teased free and he lifted it—to uncover a compartment as shallow as it was empty. He sighed and tried the other seat. The rear-seat compartment yielded hobbles, a few spare pieces of harness, and a pair of heavy straps and buckles that had no place in the four-horse harness. He studied them for a moment and then got out to study the coach again. There were scratches on the perch just forward of where it joined to the middle of the rear axle. He passed a strap through the spokes and around the perch. Everything fit. And thus, with both back wheels securely seized up, the stage began slipping and skidding down the hairpin curves of the last descent into the county seat. Even this way the horses had to step lively to keep ahead of it.

It was just plain hair raising. The edge of the cliff was not quite vertical. Somebody had, after all, managed to carve a road out of it, but the road was approximately a hand span wider than the stage, which left little room for error. Wes guessed he could jump off and possibly escape with little more than a few broken bones, but the horses had treated him decently so far, not giving him away or playing any of the little games that amuse horses when they sense that the man in charge doesn't understand all there is to know about equine moods. He braced his stiff leg and clung to the reins.

It had not occurred to Wes that the weekly arrival of the Opal stage down this embankment might be a spectacle that the whole town turned out for. But as he skidded around the final hairpin and the horses slowed and halted, it was apparent that the citizenry had turned out to see whether he was going to make it or not. Still a furlong from the nearest gawker, he unstrapped the rear wheels and tossed the gear inside the empty stage. Then he finished the drive down another single-street town, waiting to see if the horses would know where to turn in. They did.

"See you made it in one piece," the sheriff observed.

"People make bets on it?" Wes asked.

"It's the only game in town," Hurley said soberly.

"Got some more letters here," Wes said. He squinted at the envelopes. "Any idea where I might find a Mr. Polk?"

"He's about to find you," Hurley said, and turned away, presumably on urgent county business. Wes turned to face the short, puffing man who could have been a brother or cousin of Green Eyeshade up in Opal.

"Where the hell have you been?" the short man snapped.

"On a Sunday school picnic," Wes said evenly. "Your name Polk?"

"Of course I'm Polk. Now where the hell have you been all this time?"

Wes handed him the letter. "There's your stage." He began walking out of the corral, into the street. Now which way was the mercantile?

"Where do you think you're going?" the little man shrieked, his voice rising to a near soprano.

Wes hesitated a moment, then turned to face the irate Mr. Polk. "There's your stage," he said. "Five dollars got it delivered. It'll take considerably more if you want me to stand around and answer questions." The short man was still shrieking when he stepped into the street and saw the mercantile sign. As he went into the general store Wes noted that the short man had finally stopped yelling. Now he was hotfooting it off in the same direction the sheriff had disappeared.

"You must be the man brought the stage in," the clerk in the mercantile hazarded. He was a youngish man with his hair parted amidships. His attempt at a mustache was more promise than actuality. When Wes nodded, the young man continued, "Funny how you did it. Old Gabe used to come skidding all the way into town."

Wes didn't comment. The man he had picked out of the dust had seemed too old for futile bravado at the expense of his horses. And they hadn't acted as if they had been mistreated. He supposed the old man had been over the road often enough to know exactly where to let the team out. Still, Wes couldn't understand how the coach could have made the last relatively level furlong into town with wheels locked—unless somebody had whipped the daylights out of the poor horses. He tried to remember what he had come here to buy.

There was salt and matches and baking powder and corn meal and flour. But he was going to have to lug it all so the amounts were relatively small, well within the scope of the couple of dollars he had budgeted.

"Any place around here I can get a cheap gun?" he asked.

"How cheap?"

He held up the change from his gold piece.

The young man thought a moment. "Might try Ojalvo," he guessed. "He's a couple of doors down on this side of the street." Since he pronounced the *j* as in English, Wes wasn't quite sure what to look for. Then, out in the street he saw the three gilded balls and knew the proprietor of that establishment was undoubtedly Sephardic.

"Yes, I have two such rifles," Mr. Ojalvo said in precise English. "Here you see a Palmer fifty-six fifty. It uses Spencer cartridges. For two dollars and seventy cents I offer the rifle and twenty rounds." While Wes was trying not to

show his outrage at the way prices had gone up, the pawnbroker continued, "But here I have something that might
serve you better." He held out a venerable Sharps. "You
know this rifle?"

Wes did. He also doubted if he could afford it.

"This gun has been used," Ojalvo said, "but not abused.
With twenty rounds you may have it for two dollars."

Wes took the rifle to the doorway and slipped cardboard
in the breech so he could study the barrel. It was better than
he had hoped. *"Pero es mucho dinero,"* he muttered.

Ojalvo gave him a sharp look and asked a question in
some language Wes had never heard. When he shook his
head, the pawnbroker reverted to the same archaic Spanish
Wes had once learned. "You are a man of some knowledge," the pawnbroker said. "A dollar ninety?"

"How about less knowledge and a dollar fifty?"

From then on the conversation became brisk until moments later Wes stood on the street with a rifle and ammunition, his groceries, and almost a dollar left of his original
five. He fiddled with his purchases until they had been ar-
ranged into a backpack, assembled with the aid of the
binder twine used to tie them, and stepped out with the
Sharps over his shoulder. He was beginning to regret his
shortness with the officious little stationmaster, but he was
damned if he was going to go back there and try to bum a
ride. He sighed. To hell with them. He started marching.
He had not gone more than a block when the sheriff,
mounted on the same roan mare, trotted up alongside him.
"Goin' any place in particular?" he asked.

Wes resisted the impulse to tell Hurley it was none of his
business. "Got to get a crop in if I'm going to make it in this
country," he said.

Still, the sheriff walked his horse alongside while Wes
strode back out of town, heading for the switchback climb.

Even giving it his best, he knew he would be cutting it fine to make it back to his tent before dark.

"Polk wanted me to arrest you." From the way he said it Wes abruptly realized the puffy little stationmaster must be as annoying to the sheriff as he had been to Wes.

"You goin' to do it?" he asked.

"Don't believe so," the sheriff said. "First place, it won't be any problem findin' you if you're headed back on the Opal road." He paused and spoke soothingly to his mare who seemed to be feeling her oats this morning despite having climbed up and down the hair-raising road. "Second place, the way they explained this job t'me, a man's got to commit a crime first afore I can go arrestin' him."

Wes gave the lawman a curious glance. "Been a while since I heard anybody use that for an excuse," he said. "What did he want me arrested for?"

"Don't rightly know," Hurley said. "Came stompin' over all full o' fire, but when I tried to pin him down—" He shrugged. "You can't be too hard on Polk. Every time a stage gets robbed everybody blames him."

"So he's tryin' to blame me?"

The sheriff gave Wes an odd look. "Not exactly," he said. "Fact o' the matter is, he asked me to come out and apologize. Wanted me to ask you to come back in town and talk about a steady job."

Wes was so startled he stopped walking to look at the sheriff. This was twice he had been offered jobs—at a time when jobs were hard to come by. And it wasn't as if he was that much of an expert at anything around here where his field of expertise seemed to have little demand. R&D

"You sure got some funny people in this country," he remarked. "I get the feelin' I'm in the middle of something I don't know anything about."

"Now ain't that a fact," Hurley said. "Of late I often get the same feeling myself."

"How often's the stage been robbed?"

"'Bout three times in the last six months."

Wes shifted his makeshift pack on his back and lowered the Sharps from his shoulder. "So now the stage company needs a new victim?"

"Guess that's one way of putting it," the sheriff said.

"Got any idea who's doing it?" Wes had intended to turn down the offer, but with less than a dollar in his pocket, and with somewhere between ten and fifteen miles ahead of him, and a missing kneecap . . . without quite realizing what he was letting himself in for, he had already turned and was walking back down the street beside the mounted sheriff.

"Steamer finally shoalwatered its way upriver yesterday," the sheriff remarked after a few steps. "Uh, you'll find Mr. Polk's disposition somewhat improved," he added as he touched his hat brim and spurred the mare off down the street.

Which left Wes with a feeling that he had been spoken to in an unknown language. He didn't know whether he was supposed to understand it or if the man on horseback was just testing his intelligence. He was still trying to figure out just what he had missed in this whole odd business when he turned back into the stage company's corral.

The stage had been wiped clean of dust and the empty boot now bulged with luggage. In the shade of the office veranda men in heavy work clothes lounged. Abruptly the office door opened and the same Mr. Polk who had shrilled soprano at him less than an hour ago hastened out with a grin like a jackass eating thistles. "Mr. Brooks," the station agent said fulsomely, "please come inside. There are things we must discuss."

CHAPTER IV

Following the little man, Wes wondered what he had that plenty of other lean and hungry men in this country didn't have. Surely he was past the age of boyish charm. They stepped through and over the lounging men whose lack of curiosity was total, and finally they were inside an office where Wes bemusedly accepted a seat and a cigar.

"Sorry I blew up at you that way," the little man began. "I thought you'd hired on for good."

Wes waited.

"Where'd you learn to drive four-in-hand?"

"Just picked it up," Wes said. He was telling the strict truth.

"Pay's a hundred dollars a month," Polk said hopefully.

"For what?" Wes managed to conceal his astonishment.

"For driving the stage." The agent was having trouble controlling himself.

"That's not exactly what I meant," Wes said, relenting a bit. "How often, and where, and who furnishes cartridges?"

"Oh." There was a slight pause and then Wes learned he would be expected to drive the stage from here to Opal and back once a week, that he was not expected to curry horses or soothe passengers, that drivers did not handle baggage, and that, providing he got the stage from here to there in a reasonable time, Wes could manage things any way he pleased. It sounded too good to be true.

"And what about bandits?" he asked.

The small man gave him an enigmatic look and shrugged. This, Wes decided, must be why he was being offered so magnificent a wage. He wondered if the stationmaster suspected how many years he had risked his life for a damn sight less.

"Ready to go?" Polk asked.

"Reckon I ought to go buy a sidearm first."

Polk studied him a moment. "Passengers waiting," he said, then seemed to remember something. He went to the corner of the room and opened a file cabinet.

Wes studied the pistol and belt the stationmaster handed him. "Will this do?" Polk asked.

It was a double-action Army Model Colt. Wes felt it and the cylinder was not wobbly. He pulled the cartridges and checked them for tarnish. Forty-one hundredths of an inch was a respectable and familiar-sized hunk of lead. "Been fired lately?" he asked.

Polk assured him that the revolver was in perfect condition. Wes was inclined to take his word for it. He buckled it on and in the process discovered that once again he had walked off with the stage company's whip, which was still wrapped round his waist. He put it back, this time with the shot-loaded butt hanging to the left where it would not interfere with the gun.

Outside the passengers—fresh cannon fodder for the mine, he supposed—were passing a couple of bottles back and forth. He wondered if they were going to try to take his measure on the way up to Opal.

"Passengers all here and ready to leave?" he asked.

Polk nodded. "Uh, there is just one other thing," he added.

Wes waited for the other man to deal him the joker.

"Stablehand by the name of Grottman," the puffy stationmaster said. "A size sixty jumper and a number two hat."

Wes still waited. "So what's the problem?" he finally asked.

"Ed Grottman sort of thinks he was in line for the job now that Gabe's dead."

"Is he?"

"I hired you."

Wes sighed. So it was to be one of those things. He wondered what made him so attractive to this stage company. "Any other surprises?" he asked.

"I hope not. One more robbery and the mine and stage company'll both be out of business."

Wes nodded and was striding toward the stage when Polk added, "Almost forgot. You'll have a lady passenger this trip. Those muckers are a rough lot. Hope you won't mind if she rides up on the box with you."

Wes minded. Four horses were problem enough without a woman. "Providing she keeps quiet and out of the way," he muttered. He stepped outside the office and began threading his way through the lounging miners. Abruptly he realized they were not so incurious and inattentive as he had supposed. Wes could fairly feel the excitement. Though nobody moved and nobody touched him as he picked his way through the tight-packed knot of drinking men, he knew something was about to happen.

"Time to go," he said conversationally, and began climbing up to the box. Climbing with a stiff knee was not something he did well. He was going to have to study this stage for footholds and work out something better than this awkward hand-over-hand scaling of the front wheel.

"Passengers ride inside." The voice was low and dangerous. As Wes's face topped the box and met another face coming up the opposite side of the stage he knew he had just made acquaintance with Ed Grottman. He remembered

Polk's description. Size sixty jumper and number two hat was about all that could be said for the whiskey-pickled whiskery face that glared at him from across the box.

"Sorry," Wes said. "But I'm not a passenger. You'll have to step down now."

"Let's see you make me."

"Sorry again," Wes said, still pulling himself up until he was able to get a foot on top of the wheel. "But I'm tryin' to break myself of the habit of making people do things." He continued climbing and was now high enough to get a decent foothold.

Ed Grottman was not bluffing worth a damn. He had been climbing too, and as his huge muscular body came into view Wes knew he was in for it. Given two good legs he could probably box this grotesque giant into exhaustion. But he didn't have two legs and if Grottman were ever to get those gorilla arms around him . . .

Wes still gripped the stationmaster's cigar in his teeth. Which reminded him that the short man had given him something else, courtesy of the company. He studied the irate giant who faced him across the width of the box, wondering how much intelligence there was inside a number two hat. "Do you know your own name?" he asked. It was not a question calculated to inspire lasting friendship.

"I know my name," the giant replied. "And I know yours too. It's gonna be mud."

Wes decided the other man had passed his intelligence test. "Do you know what this is?" Abruptly the giant was looking into a hole forty-one hundredths of an inch across.

"That ain't fair," Grottman grumbled.

"You're damn right it isn't," Wes agreed. "But it's smart. Now let's see if you're smart enough to figure out what next."

"You're going to pay for this," Grottman grumbled. But he wasted no time dropping down off the box.

It had happened so quickly that the waiting miners didn't quite realize it was all over until they saw Wes leisurely holstering the Colt. He was gathering up reins and the miners were clambering into the coach when abruptly Wes realized he had forgotten something else. Better finish what he'd started, he guessed. "Mr. Grottman," he called.

The giant turned to glare at him from red-rimmed eyes.

"My pack and rifle inside the office," Wes said. "Would you please bring them here?"

Grottman stared unbelieving for a moment, then turned and lurched into the office. He came out a moment later holding pack and rifle as if they might explode at any moment. Wes sat on the box, the Colt holstered. "Up here, please," he said.

The giant's eyes darted from the rifle he held to the Colt Wes did not. Then Grottman did perhaps the most intelligent thing he ever did in his life. Wordlessly, he handed rifle and pack up to Wes. "Thank you," Wes said.

Grottman did not answer.

Wes was sorting out the reins, hoping the horses would not pick this moment to make a fool of him, when a woman appeared in the gateway to the corral. Damn! He'd almost forgotten he was to have a woman passenger. He was sorting out his bad knee for the easiest way down when the short station agent came puffing out of his office to help the young lady up onto the box beside Wes.

She was clad in a twill traveling suit that, in the style of the decade, was cut generously enough to prevent any gentleman of proper upbringing from thinking improper thoughts or seeing so much as an instep to inspire such thoughts. Wordlessly, Wes caught her arm and helped her up over the wheel and onto the box beside him. Despite the

voluminous traveling suit, this young lady managed it somewhat more nimbly than Wes could.

"Mr. Brooks," Polk began officiously, "Miss Upton."

Since he was already gripping her elbow Wes deemed the
familiarities sufficient. He nodded, but obviously the short
man expected more. Wes was damned if he could guess
what. "Got your traps all aboard, Miss Upton?" he asked.

Miss Upton said "Yes," and there was no excuse for further delay. He finished unwrapping reins from the brake
pole and sorting them out. With a silent prayer to the gods
of propriety, he rattled the reins and clucked. The horses
did not let him down.

They trotted briskly out of the corral, swinging wide, and
the heavily laden stage did not come close to tipping. Miss
Upton sat quietly on the left side of the box, as composed as
if she always rode this way. Perhaps, he decided, she was
afraid any outburst might get her sent down to ride inside
with the half-dozen unwashed passengers jammed into the
coach.

The horses' brief enthusiasm died as they tackled the
winding switchbacks he had slipped and skidded down less
than two hours ago. Stage company ought to have switched
teams, he thought. Then he realized there must be only one
team. If the stage had arrived on schedule yesterday evening
the horses would have been fed and rested by now. And so
would he. Nevertheless, he tried to ignore the emptiness in
his midsection.

"Isn't that an odd way to carry a whip, Mr. Brooks?"

Wes glanced from the laboring horses to the young
woman who sat beside him. Miss Upton's attire was less
revealing than that of other eras, but she was young and
seemingly possessed no gross defects. Her skin was fair and
would soon be freckled, Wes suspected, unless she were to
either get indoors or trade that pillbox hat for something

with a brim. Beneath the hat she wore abundant quantities of red hair.

"The whip," she reminded.

"What about it?"

"You may be called on to use it before long," Miss Upton said.

Wes wondered if this young lady might possibly know more about horses than he did. It wouldn't be difficult, he decided. There were any number of ways he could make a fool of himself and/or reveal how little he knew about driving a four-in-hand. The quickest way would be to go shooting his mouth off. Wordlessly, he gathered the reins into his left hand and began unwrapping the whip from around his waist. There ought to be a place to hang it, but he couldn't find any. He coiled it and put the braided rawhide on the seat between them.

Meanwhile the horses were dragging the coach perilously close to the edge of the narrow road. Below them he could see the county seat. If the coach were to go off this track he could be back there in less time than it took to think about it. He yelled and slapped reins and the stage edged back away from danger.

"New, aren't you?" the girl was asking.

Wes nodded.

"Are you expecting bandits this trip?"

He shrugged.

"Hardly likely," the girl added. "Valuable cargo must all come in the other direction."

His empty stomach churned. Why hadn't he demanded an advance on his salary? Why hadn't he gotten something to eat before committing himself to this all-day drive back up to Opal? It would be noon before he was even in sight of his tent, and there was nothing ready to eat there—nor could he expect to have a job very long if he were to make Miss Upton and all those other passengers cool their heels while he fixed himself lunch. He sighed and looked away from the girl long enough to yawn. He wondered if she could hear the rumbling of his empty stomach.

The horses were sweating mightily as they labored around the next switchback. As near as he could work it out, they were about halfway up. Once more a wheel came perilously close to the edge. Beneath the stage a rock came loose and went skittering down toward the county seat. For some time now there had been no noise at all inside the stage. Wes was stricken with a sudden inspiration. He whoaed the horses and put his boot on the brake.

"Goin' to get a little chancy from here on up!" he called. "Anybody want to get out and walk to the top?" Immediately the white-knuckled passengers boiled out the door that faced the nearly vertical wall. While the horses rested, the men began climbing the switchback road, struggling to whistle and horseplay. Wes supposed it was even more frightening from inside, with less chance to jump. He glanced at the girl, but Miss Upton did not seem inclined to walk.

When the horses were blown, he slapped reins and clucked the stage back into motion. Beside him, the girl sat straight, the tips of her boots showing beneath her voluminous twill skirt. Wes wondered if she would be so confident if she knew how little he knew about horses.

It wasn't as if he was totally ignorant, he tried to tell himself. After all, he'd grown up on a farm, had plowed and harrowed. But that had been nineteen years ago and with a two-horse team. What on earth was the proper way to hold the reins driving four-in-hand? "Ever drive?" he asked the girl.

"Somewhat more than you have, I suspect," Miss Upton said. "Tell me, Mr. Brooks, how did you happen to take up this line of work?"

CHAPTER V

If he were a younger and more confiding type of man Wes guessed he might have chosen that moment to confess his ignorance. He reflected ruefully that at this time yesterday he had not even dreamed of driving a stagecoach. Now he was fair caught, seduced by the prospect of a steady income again.

"It's a living," he said. "Man's got to do something with his life."

The road turned narrower at this point, barely wide enough for the stage's wheels. If he'd gone down as slowly as they were going up, Wes guessed he might have chickened out and gotten down to walk beside—but there wasn't room for that. A prudent man might prefer to walk ahead, leading the horses.

But horses were not that different from men and either species could be totally demoralized by any hint of weakness in those they trusted. His attention was on the horses who seemed to understand that this stretch was particularly dangerous. Despite blinders the animals nearest the precipice crowded their mates, struggling to put some distance between themselves and infinity. Which was fine with Wes since it put the creaking coach six inches farther from that crumbling bank. Beside him the girl was squirming and doing something. He concentrated on holding the reins—just holding them, suspecting the horses, as usual, understood the situation better than he and would handle things by themselves as long as they could preserve that belief in him that horses share with dogs concerning the omniscience and benevolence of man, the divine animal.

Then, as the bank crumbled beneath a rear wheel and the coach lurched toward eternity Wes discovered within himself the need for a benevolent protector of some superior species. But, yelling and shaking the reins, he was too busy to create new theologies. Aid came from an unexpected source as the whip cracked over the head of the lead horses who put their all into it, and an instant later the coach was back on relatively level ground. "Thanks," Wes muttered between clenched teeth.

Miss Upton nodded gravely as she concerned herself with stringing out the whip behind them along the canvas roof of the mud wagon. They were catching up with the walking miners, who showed no inclination to board the stage until they reached the top of this grade. Nor was there room to pass. Wes halted the horses and set the brake again to give the walking men a head start. The horses blew gratefully.

"You may be a man of many talents," Miss Upton said, "but driving is not one of them. Why were you selected for this job?"

"Beats me," Wes said. He wondered if this self-contained young woman was going to get him fired before he had a chance to learn his job. Who was she anyhow? Why was a woman like this heading for a town like Opal? Surely she didn't belong to that sisterhood of women who dwelt in tumbledown houses at the lower edge of town.

"Will you be annoyed if I try to explain something?" Miss Upton asked.

"In my position I'll take any explanations I can get," Wes said.

The horses were blown by now and the half dozen miners were within a hundred yards of the top of the grade. The girl reached across Wes and untied the reins. "This way," she said, and began gathering them in her gloved hands.

Wes had been holding the reins in separate bunches of rights and lefts. He wondered momentarily if the girl understood all she knew when she gathered the entire fistful into her left hand. She held it close to her breast, with the near leader's reins uppermost between her forefinger and the off leader's reins beneath. Between her middle finger the wheel horses' reins were grouped in the same way. It wasn't until she cracked the whip that he saw how neatly she controlled all the horses with one hand, slipping reins back and forth through her fingers until all horses were pulling evenly. "So that's how it's done," he mused.

Rounding the next switchback, she looped the leaders' reins under her thumb and pointed the horses. For the first time the stage rounded a curve without that grinding, sideways motion on the front wheels that Wes had considered normal. He wondered where Miss Upton had mastered this technique. But even more he wondered when he would ever find time to eat again.

"Are you a mining man, Mr. Brooks?"

"Not so's you'd notice," Wes said, intent on Miss Upton's hands. It was amazing how much more willingly the horses were working now that somebody was communicating properly.

By now the passengers had walked to the top of the grade and disappeared. He hoped they weren't as hungry as he was. Heads down, the horses struggled to drag the Abbott, Downing & Co. Celerity Coach up the rutted incline. Throughout the West this lighter, four-horse Celerity Coach was known as a mud wagon. At least he wasn't struggling with a six-horse Concord.

But Wes wasn't struggling at all. Miss Upton still drove. They topped the rise and the miner passengers came into sight lounging beside the dusty track. Hastily, she tried to hand the reins to him. "I ain't proud," Wes said. "You want to drive some more I'll be happy to watch."

The girl gave him an odd look and coaxed the sweating horses to a halt while the miners got back in. Several of them stared at the girl who still held the reins, but they refrained from comment. Wes had once read that back East where stages were a thing of the past the rich dudes had taken to getting up coaching parties where people drove for the fun of it. This, he guessed, must be where the capable Miss Upton had mastered the art.

With the miners back inside she cracked the whip—without actually touching the horses with it, he noted, and once more the canvas-topped mud wagon was jolting away toward the creek where the old man in whiskers and buckskins had drawn down on him yesterday. He wondered what the old geezer had been expecting to find inside the empty stage. The horses slowed to ford the creek and—there was the old man again.

This time he was not pointing a rifle at them. While the horses drank, the girl passed the reins over for Wes to tie to the brake pole. The old man came close and squinted. "You be Miss Alberdeen?" he inquired.

"Yes, Mr. Bridges," the girl replied gravely. "You haven't changed a bit."

"You have." From the way he said it, the old man obviously approved of the changes.

Wes found himself wondering once again just who this competent young woman was. There were only two kinds of girls who went to mining camps. She did not belong to one category, which left only the other. He sighed. Tonight over dinner she would casually remark to her father that the new driver didn't know beans about horses and that would be the end of Wes's bonanza once the owner's daughter told the truth about him. Should have lied to her, he guessed. But it would have been impossible to conceal from this observant young lady all the things he didn't know about horses. Tomorrow he would be back on his diggings trying to get in a crop.

Meanwhile the horses had drunk and rested, the whiskered and buckskinned Mr. Bridges had tipped his hat, and the stage was ready to roll. Wes untied the reins and managed to get them into his left fist the way the girl had. He didn't want to risk cutting a horse until he'd had a while to practice with that whip so he got them moving in his usual way by yelling and shaking the reins. It was amazing how much easier it went with the reins all in one hand, the other free for adjusting tension and pointing the lead team around corners.

"You learn swiftly, Mr. Brooks," the girl remarked.

"I hope so," he muttered.

The girl turned to look squarely at him, swirling abundant quantities of red hair. She changed her mind with equal abruptness and didn't ask whatever was on her mind.

"Carrying any valuables?" Wes asked.

This time the girl didn't turn to face him. "Why?" she asked.

Wordlessly Wes nodded. It wasn't the way he had been expecting it. Hadn't been expecting it at all really, he guessed. Stages coming down from Opal might be carrying something worth the effort of a holdup. But heading up from Okapogum? There might be a couple of dollars in the miners' pockets. Wes had less than a dollar in his. The stage didn't even carry a strongbox. Still, there were four men on horses a half mile up the road. They didn't look like passengers.

"Oh dear!" Miss Upton gasped. "Do you suppose they're bandits?"

Wes shrugged. Fording the creek would have been the logical spot for a holdup. But that seemed to be the ancient's—Bridges, she had called him—spot. Did they sell franchises for different stretches of road? "Miss Upton," he began, "I've no wish to pry into affairs that are none of my business, but you seem to know your way about this country better than I. Do you know those men up ahead? Have you any reason to believe their intentions might be pacific?"

"What an odd turn of phrase," the girl murmured.

"Yes," Wes said impatiently. "One falls into odd habits living on islands amid that most peculiarly named ocean. But what of the more urgent peculiarity of that quartet ahead of us?"

"I don't know."

"Would you like to get down inside?"

"No, Mr. Brooks. But perhaps it would be better if I were to drive and let you handle other problems."

It sounded like the best idea Wes had heard all day. He handed Miss Upton the reins and began looking to his weapons.

Should have fired the Colt, he guessed. But he couldn't do it while driving and hadn't been able to bring himself to spook the horses while the young lady held the reins. He checked the cylinder and it was, as he already knew, fully loaded. He made sure there was ammunition in the Sharps.

Meanwhile the four men on horseback became gradually more distinct as the stage rocked on toward the place where they waited, two on each side of the road.

There should be some sort of protocol. A shot over their bows? There was always the odd chance that they were four law-abiding citizens with legitimate business—a letter to mail, a message for somebody in Opal—perhaps even some news about the real bandits. In the pig's eye.

But Wes knew that he was not going to fire the first shot.

He wondered irrelevantly if the inside passengers even knew the stage was about to be halted. Not that it made any difference. If they had a gun between them they were probably too drunk to use it.

The four men wore broad-brimmed Stetsons in the Texas style, which was unusual this far north. Their horses and saddles were the nondescript catmeat that could be found corralled next to the bunkhouse of any ranch in these parts. The only unusual thing was all four of them were armed with six guns and rifles. But the rifles were all in saddle boots, Colts in holsters. They were loaded for bear and Wes knew they could cover him in less time than it took to think about it but . . . they hadn't—so far. Much as every instinct told him to even up the odds and get his blow in first, he couldn't do it. Nobody had drawn on him. And besides, there was the girl. Miss Upton—had the grizzled old man called her Alberdeen? Gripping the reins like a pack of cards, close to the vest of her twill traveling suit, she sat on the left side of the box. If he were to start shooting, Miss Upton was sure to get hit.

"What's the problem?" he asked as the girl drew the stage to a halt.

"Where is it?" The tallest of the quartet was a slim man somewhat younger than Wes, with yellow hair, a yellow buckskin shirt and even yellowish eyes in his expressionless face.

Wes had seen that kind of face before. He hadn't the slightest idea what the yellow-haired man wanted.

"You ridin' the stage or just wastin' company time?" Wes asked.

"Where is it?" Yellow Hair was insistent if nothing else.

"Perhaps if you could tell us exactly what it is you're looking for," Miss Upton began in reasoning tones.

"You jes' keep your trap shut!" Yellow Hair snapped

without looking at her. Eyes fixed on Wes, he once more demanded, "What'd you do with it?"

Wes sighed. Yellow Hair and his friends apparently didn't want a ride on the stage. "I ain't sure exactly what you want," Wes drawled. "Could it be this?" He didn't seem to be moving with any particular speed, but the Colt was in his hand and pointing at Yellow Hair before that man could touch rifle or pistol. Lest there be some unfortunate accident, Wes pulled the trigger twice.

CHAPTER VI

Despite the booming of .41-caliber ammunition, Wes heard a swish past his ear. For an instant he thought a bullet had missed him, but it was the girl popping the whip lash in a dark-haired man's face. Man and horse reared simultaneously backward and went down together in a welter of kicking legs. Wes was struggling to get a shot at a third member of the quartet of outlaws when the girl's whip popped again, this time over the lead team's heads and the stage was rocketing away, leaving behind one dead yellow-haired man, one dark-haired man with a cut face and possible injuries from his own horse, plus two also-rans who had not gotten off a shot between them. The also-rans were also running.

It was half a mile before the horses settled down to a trot and the girl could turn to face Wes who had improved on the interval by punching the empties out of his Colt and reloading. "Now I see why you got the job," she said thoughtfully.

Wes considered her explanation. It didn't make sense. He hadn't even possessed a pistol when he was hired for this job. Nobody could have guessed he knew how to use one. He had the feeling that an opportunity had been lost. If the girl hadn't whipped up the horses, surely the sight of their two most aggressive members out of action might have loosened the tongues of the other two. If these weren't the same bandits who'd gotten old Gabe and the strongbox yesterday morning—but if they were . . . Wes sighed. There were just too many things he didn't know or understand. What, he wondered, had Yellow Hair wanted? If he had brains to rob a stagecoach, he ought to know enough not to bother with stages heading this way and carrying nothing of value.

"They teach you to use a whip like that in one of those coaching clubs back East?" he asked.

The girl stared at Wes for a moment, then wordlessly handed him the reins. By now the horses had settled down to their customary trot and the road was as smooth as it would ever get. While he struggled to acquire that indefinable quality that horsemen call hands, the stage rocked over the flat toward his diggings. If he didn't hang around home more and cook a few more meals, that camp-robbing whiskey jack was going to move on toward better pickings.

Instead of answering his question, the girl countered with one of her own. "What was it they wanted from you?"

"Beats me," Wes said. He pointed a mile ahead where the ridgepole of his tent was just coming into view. "That's home. Do I look rich enough to be worth robbing?"

The girl looked silently from Wes to the tent.

As the trotting horses came nearer, Wes could see something was wrong. He sensed the girl studying him. Inside the stage the passengers were finally quieting down, as they realized nobody was going to stop long enough to tell them what all the shooting was about. But when Wes finally reined up before his tent, they all came boiling out to stretch their legs and ask, "Who lives here? Oh, you live here? Why live way out here? Somebody got it in for you?"

Somebody apparently had. Wes's tent was slashed to useless ribbons. Somebody had flattened the tin stove with a head-sized boulder. His meager supplies of flour and cornmeal had been scattered so wide even the whiskey jack would have his work cut out to make a meal from them. Everything he owned had been destroyed except his blankets, and they were gone.

Miss Upton came down from the box to stand in silent sympathy while he surveyed the mess. "Well, Mr. Brooks," she said, "whatever it is they think you have, they've spared no effort looking for it."

He nodded. The ax handle was broken, but the blade was still good. They had used it to put a hole through the bottom of his water bucket.

The miners sensed that this was a moment to leave a man alone with his possibly dangerous thoughts. They moseyed around to the opposite side of the coach and began sharing out their single remaining bottle.

"May I help in any way?" the girl asked. "Perhaps there's some keepsake they missed?"

Wes shook his head. "They were nineteen bad years," he said, "*Y basta.*" Wordlessly, he slung the broken-handled ax up onto the roof of the mud wagon. He went around to the off side and began his awkward shinny up the brake pole until he could swing around and sit on the box.

"Not even a letter or a girl's picture?" she probed.

"Especially not."

Miss Upton at this point wisely decided not to pursue the subject. They drove silently away toward the foothills that concealed Opal, past the place where he had found old Gabe dead. Old Gabe, at least, was no longer suffering. Now that he was over the first gut-wrenching anger at the sight of his ruined camp, Wes once more had time to calculate how many hours it had been since last he had eaten.

The sun was already halfway down the afternoon sky. If they made it into Opal before dark, he might be able to find accommodation of some sort there. By then it would be something over thirty hours since his last meal.

But he wasn't hungry now. In thirty-seven years on this

imperfect planet he had learned that laws, like every other human invention, partake of the imperfections of their makers. Four strangers had done him dirt for no particular reason. Or had there been a reason?

He reviewed the timetable of events. Thirty hours ago he'd been minding his own business, struggling to reassemble the shreds of his life. Since then he'd picked up a dead stage driver, had delivered letters to the county seat, had managed to acquire an enemy in Opal. And he couldn't even remember the name of the mucker whose nose he'd flattened.

Could that be it?

Reluctantly, Wes decided it was not. Those four bandits had accused him of hiding something, knowing something. Unless he was guessing wrong, the mucker in Opal wouldn't even know where Wes lived. But somebody had taken enough interest in his affairs to ferret out that knowledge. Twenty-five per cent of that group was no longer dangerous. But there were still the two also-rans who had run away—plus a man with a cut face and possibly a missing eye if the girl's whip had been accurate enough. The girl was saying something.

"Uh—what?"

"You were working on an island in the Pacific?" she repeated.

"Under long-term contract."

"Was it dangerous work?"

Wes shrugged.

"More dangerous than driving a stage from Okapogum to Opal?"

"I couldn't say," Wes said tiredly. "You must remember, Miss Upton, that I'm a stranger here. I've no idea what I'm getting into. Matter of fact, I don't even know where you fit in."

"Rather awkwardly, I'm afraid," the girl said. "My father's manager of the mine."

"Oh." Wes supposed he ought to be giving Miss Upton the deference her exalted station demanded. But he was just too wrung out from one damned thing after another and all on an empty stomach. "Home for a vacation and to see how the other half lives?" As he said it he knew the tone was not as light as it might have been.

So, apparently, did Miss Upton. "You sound bitter, Mr. Brooks," she said. "But at least you had a chance."

There was enough truth in this for Wes not to answer.

"What," the girl continued, "what if you'd been born into a different skin—given the best education available, prepared to make your mark in the world—and then learned there were no openings at present, none tomorrow—none for as far in the future as anyone can foresee?"

"What'd you want to be?" Wes wondered. "A trick rider in the circus?"

"No, Mr. Brooks. All I ever wanted to do is what any dutiful son does as a matter of course."

"Leave Paw with one less mouth to feed? You ain't so bad lookin' you couldn't manage that."

"Mr. Brooks, must you be deliberately obtuse?"

"Sorry. But I put my trust in a father who didn't do that well by me. Guess I should have known better. Great White Father can't keep his word with Indians or Filipinos, why should anybody expect him to play straight with white men?"

"So that was the island."

Wes slipped an inch of the off leader's reins through his fingers and rattled them over his back. The horse's head went down and his traces came taut again.

"You must have lost something precious there."

"I'll make up a list for you someday." They couldn't be more than two or three miles from Opal by now. He had his scant bundle of provisions stashed beneath his feet. But since the vandals had worked over his possessions, he didn't have so much as a pot to cook in, nor the slightest hint of a roof over his head. "Your father's the principal stockholder in the mine?"

"When last I heard from him."

"And does the mine own the stage company?"

"Probably. There was no reason for a stage until the mine became workable."

Wes was about to ask the girl if she could prevail on somebody to get him an advance in salary—enough to put up at a boardinghouse somewhere in Opal until time to take the next stage down to the river when abruptly he realized what the girl had said. "When last you heard from him?" he echoed. "And when was that?"

Abruptly there was a *feeling*. Wes braced himself unconsciously. The horses' ears pricked up and a moment later he knew it was the pressure wave from a blast up at the mine. There was very little noise—just a rumbling growl from deep in the earth, but he felt his ears ring for a moment and then the horses were galloping.

Wes studied the road ahead—a mile of straight climb toward the bottom of Opal—and let them gallop. Beside him, the girl clung to the box with both hands, showing the toes of her boots beneath her twill skirt. "Do you understand about cooling horses out?" she finally asked.

Wes did. But he also suspected they would work off their nervousness soon enough galloping uphill. As if on cue the lathered horses slowed to a broken paced trot and moments later were walking the final mile up the creek-divided single street of Opal.

There had been no whistles for the last hour or so. Late afternoon sun glared in their eyes as the mud wagon climbed toward the final turn into the corral. The streets were practically empty save for a few slatternly appearing

women out haggling for necessities. Nearing the café where
he had been accosted yesterday, he saw a blank oriental
face staring from an open doorway. As usual, he was not
quite sure if the Chinese was looking at him or at something
a thousand years beyond him.

Then up near the arched entry into the stage company
corral he saw another face framed in black braids. The boy
waved and Wes waved back, realizing he should have asked
the Indian boy his name.

Wes was going to have to start paying more attention to
faces in this town—if he still had a job here.

"First the leaders, then the wheelers," Miss Upton murmured. "That way you won't grind so much iron off the
front tires."

Wes concentrated on pointing the horses and this time
the coach made a less spectacular entrance into the corral.
He was tying reins to the brake pole and trying to devise
some less awkward way to get down off the box when the
green-eyeshaded agent came from the doorway of the office.

Wes slid to the ground and walked around to the near
side to help Miss Upton down off the box. She accepted his
hand, but even in her tentlike traveling skirt the girl was
more nimble than Wes. And either of her legs, he suspected,
would be infinitely more attractive than the best of his. He
put such dangerous thoughts out of his mind and was con-
centrating on the best way to buffalo some money out of the
station manager without letting that green-eyeshaded shy-
lock know how badly he needed it when abruptly the short
puffy little man was in front of him, staring at Wes and at
Miss Upton. To Wes it seemed as if his face were almost as
green as his eyeshade.

"You!" the little man wheezed.

Wes wondered if it was Miss Upton or himself who was
responsible for the prolonged wheezing oooooo of that *you*.

CHAPTER VII

But if Green Eyeshade was discomfited by the appearance of either of them, he recovered quickly, herding the drunk but docile miners into a group that the Indian boy led up the street, presumably to a company bunkhouse. Each of the miners reclaimed a bindle from the boot, which left a medium-sized steamer trunk and two Gladstones of alligator leather. There was little doubt who the trunk and matched bags belonged to.

Conditions of employment were that the driver of the Opal stage was under no obligation to handle passengers' luggage. But, Wes reflected, the passengers were also under no obligation to teach him how to drive. The trunk could wait. He fished the grips from the near-empty boot and faced Miss Upton.

Together they trudged out of the corral and up Opal's single street toward the mine. Somehow he had been expecting a robber baron's palace in steamboat gothic but the place to which the girl led him was unprepossessing. It was several doors closer to the headframe, whistles, and the general dirty confusion of the mine. The front of the building seemed to be the office of the Opal Mine and Development Company. It was only when she led him down a narrow side walkway that he discovered this was also the general manager and principal stockholder's living quarters.

The living quarters were empty or, at least, responded to no amount of knocking. The girl produced a key and led the way into the empty house. Wes had done his best uphill with a grip in each hand. By dint of some teeth gritting, he had taught himself to manage short distances without limping. But the two grips had made him sweat despite the coolness of the evening.

Miss Upton apparently did not notice as she took the grips from him and placed them in a corner beside a horsehair sofa. "And this," she said evenly, "is how the other half lives."

Wes nodded, wondering if this girl was also a mind reader. Wordlessly, he turned on his good leg and left, closing the door behind him. Back out in the street he saw the boy. The boy's surprise was just fulsome enough for Wes to know the young Indian had been waiting for him. "You know," he began, "it'd make things simpler if you had a name."

"It sure would," the boy said.

Wes studied the youngster a moment. Either the boy had forfeited his right to a name by living outside his tribe—or perhaps a name was a secret between a man and his gods. "But I've got to call you something," he decided. "How about Tinacling?"

"What's that mean?"

"It's a kind of a dance," Wes explained, remembering how nimbly the boy had scooted down the street avoiding all obstacles. "The dancers keep hopping in and out of a couple of poles that're being banged together. Miss a step and you end up with a broken ankle."

"Sounds crazy," the boy said. "Do white men do things like that?"

"No," Wes muttered. "The games white men play are much more dangerous."

"They want you back at the depot," the boy said.

Uphill a whistle let go with marrow-melting shrillness. In

another minute or two the street would be full of miners. In another minute or two Wes's stomach would have lost all memory of what it was like to eat. He followed the boy back down to the stage depot. Green Eyeshade and the company bull in the too-small derby were waiting. "What happened?" the company bull asked.

Wes glanced behind him, but the boy had already disappeared. He captured a cane-bottomed chair and lowered himself, searching for some less painful way to extend his right leg. "Starting with the sixth day of Creation?" he asked. "Or would you like to narrow it down a little?"

"Five dollars seems to go farther than it used to," Green Eyeshade said. He glanced at a corner of the office and Wes saw that somebody had off-loaded his newly acquired Sharps and his bundle of supplies from the stage. But both men's eyes were on the Colt he wore.

"Company property," Wes said. "It goes with the job."

"Job?" both men echoed.

It took Wes an instant to realize that, though these men had sent letters by him to Okapogum, the man who had hired him down there had sent nothing in return. He explained briefly that he was on the payroll until further notice. "At a hundred dollars a month," he concluded.

Twin looks of outrage and despair.

"Sounded a little steep t'me," Wes agreed. "But that was before I learned this stage gets held up at least once every trip. Might save the company money if you put me on piecework—like maybe a hundred dollars a head?"

Neither of his listeners was amused. There was a long silence and Wes became nearly as puzzled as Green Eyeshade and the company bull seemed to be.

"You killed one of them?" the bull finally asked.

Wes nodded. "And if you find some dark-haired dude

around town with a whiplash cut across his face, you might look into his background," he added.

"Why didn't you bring in the body?"

"There were two more of them. You may not value my hide very highly, but Miss Upton seems well regarded in these parts. She was there too."

"You got any idea what they wanted?"

Wes shrugged, then was struck by a sudden inspiration. "You ever bring payroll money up this way?"

"Not over once a year or so," the company bull said.

This verified Wes's opinion of company towns. Wages come and wages go, but indebtedness to the company store goes on forever. "By the way," he asked. "Who's the boss around here—you or the man down in Okapogum?"

For a moment Green Eyeshade didn't seem to hear the question. Wes pondered the change that had come over the officious little man since last he had seen him. The station agent came to with a start. "You're hired until further notice," he said.

"Unless I decide to quit."

"What?" Both men's consternation was complete.

"A day ago I was a stranger in this country—without a friend in the world," Wes explained. "And today, thanks to taking this job, I still don't have any friends, but I've sure got a sufficiency of enemies."

Either they didn't know what he was talking about or both men were consummate actors.

Wes explained about the housewarming that had wiped out his homestead. "What I was getting at," he continued, "is, this stage seems to be a once-a-week affair. Do I cool my heels all week here or back in Okapogum?"

Green Eyeshade and the man in the too-small derby glanced at one another. "Here," Green Eyeshade hastened. "By all means, spend your free time here. It may not seem much of a town, but there's hunting and fishing—all sorts of things to keep a man busy. In fact, if time hangs too heavily you might even hire on as bouncer. There're several saloons could use a man of your talents. Especially since you could probably use a little extra money now to get yourself a new outfit."

"Mr. Brooks?" The voice came from behind him.

"What the hell do you want?" the company bull snapped.

It was Tinacling. The Indian boy stood in the half-open doorway. "Mr. Upton wants to see you if you aren't too busy," the boy said.

"Oh! Of course. Can't keep Mr. Upton waiting." It was practically a chorus.

And thus Wes once more found himself on the street. It was turning dark now and miners wandered from saloon to saloon, crowding each other off the walks and into the brown-foamed creek. Somehow Tinacling danced his way between the lumbering giants, always half a step away from collision and disaster as he guided Wes back up to the Opal Mining and Development Company office. This time they went in through the front door where, behind a grillwork worthy of any bank, a thin, balding man in sleeve protectors sat at a rolltop desk.

"Thanks," he said, and handed the boy two bits. Tinacling thanked him and disappeared as the worn-looking man opened a door through the grillwork and motioned Wes into a chair. "So you're the man who saved my daughter's life," he said thoughtfully.

It was nice of her to put it that way, Wes decided. To his way of thinking, it had been more of a cooperative venture.

"Mr. Brooks," Upton continued, "I'm sure you're getting tired of telling this story but . . ." He shrugged. "People sometimes tell me less than the truth. Not that they're deliberately lying but . . . I know something's wrong. Bandits are robbing the stage practically at their own convenience, and people still tell me only what they think I might want to hear. Would you mind going over it from the beginning?"

Wes minded. He had managed to put his hunger into the back of his mind, but now there were unmistakable smells coming from the rear of the house. He had something less than a dollar in cash left over to last until his first pay day. Enough food to fill the void in his midsection would use up the better part of it. But he managed to contain his impatience long enough to fill Upton in on how he had been hired to drive the stage back and deliver some letters, how it had turned into a permanent job, and so on. He didn't bother with recounting his adventures with the quartet of stage robbers, assuming Miss Upton had already provided her father with a suitable version of that incident. He had just about wound down when he remembered the grizzled ancient who had drawn down on him and searched the stage.

"Bridges," the manager mused. "You know, he discovered this mine."

"Oh?"

"I grubstaked him," Upton explained. "Mr. Bridges bears me no grudge."

"How many people do?"

"I wish I knew," Upton said. "Any man in business is bound to make a few enemies. Times I've been tempted to hand the whole disaster over to the goddam anarchists and see if they can make a go of it any better than I can."

Smells of frying meat emanated from the rear of the premises. Wes swallowed and tried to think about something else. Upton seemed a decent enough old gaffer, for a capitalist. But if Wes didn't get out of here, get something into his stomach, he knew he was going to turn downright uncivil.

"You realize that with the country full of bandits a prudent man learns all he can about any stranger in the country," Upton was saying.

Wes could see that this might be reasonable.

"You're about the age to have left the army on half pay," the balding man continued. "You seem to have suffered some slight injury. You are not a boozer, nor do you seem enslaved to vicious habits. Yet the postmaster assures everyone within listening distance that you do not receive a pension check."

While Wes was considering what measures could be taken against that busybody of a letter sorter, Upton continued, "Has it never occurred to you that a man with your background arouses the curiosity of just about everyone in a sparsely settled territory like this?"

It had. "I suppose that's why I'm being paid a hundred dollars a month," Wes said. "So you can keep your eye on me until you decide I'm not the man who's robbing your stage."

The balding mine manager regarded him in silence.

"And since I just got wiped out of everything I own, thanks to takin' this job, it wouldn't be all that smart for me to go giving you some kind of story about all the years I spent as a Methodist missionary doing my best to bring the downtrodden heathen into the fold, now would it?"

Upton almost laughed, but at that moment a door in the rear of the office opened and Miss Upton appeared. She had removed the jacket of the twill traveling suit and replaced it with an apron. "It's ready," she said.

Upton stood and gestured for Wes to precede him into the other room. The table was set for three. It was the last thing on earth that Wes had expected, there being a line as invisible as it was uncrossable in the world where he had spent the last nineteen years of his life. Here he was in a capitalist's home, being invited to sit down at the same table with him and his daughter. It was unbelievable. But so was the smell of the food.

"I hope you like it, Mr. Brooks," Miss Upton said gravely. "It's been some time since I've had a chance to cook."

"You did this yourself?" Wes surveyed the venison steaks, the biscuits, the mounds of potatoes, and the minor lake of gravy.

"Sit down and enjoy it," Upton said heavily. "I only wish you could be as confident of collecting your hundred dollars a month."

CHAPTER VIII

Wes was so hungry that even that chilling remark could not blunt his appetite. He struggled to maintain some semblance of civilized behavior as he ingested venison, potatoes, gravy, biscuits, all the delights he had longed for. Upton ate sparingly. As the first fine edge of his appetite was blunted, Wes noted that the girl did not bother with any ladylike "eat like a bird" airs. She had been traveling too and, he abruptly realized, might have gone hungry nearly as long as he. Finally he put down the sterling knife and fork with the wheat sheaf-design and finished his third cup of coffee. "Why won't I get paid?" he asked. "Am I fired already?"

Upton shook his head. "Know anything about the mining business?" he asked.

"I don't even know what you're mining here."

"Tomorrow, if you've time, I'll have somebody show you," Upton said. He passed a napkin over his bald spot and sighed. "We're getting robbed too often. People think a gold mine is—a gold mine. Sometimes it is. But this mine's already gone broke once. Wouldn't be operating now if somebody hadn't invented a new cyaniding process to work low-grade ores."

There was a knocking, as if someone were pounding on the street door with a baseball bat. Upton sighed and excused himself to go answer the door.

Wes faced the red-haired Miss Upton across the table. "I

see you didn't give me away," he said. "It's difficult to believe such charity doesn't evaporate over a hot stove."

Abruptly Miss Upton's face was nearly as red as her hair. Wes wondered what he had said wrong. He concentrated on his coffee cup and tried not to notice her discomfiture.

"For a presumably uneducated man," the girl said thoughtfully, "you display some disconcerting lapses into literacy."

Wes laughed. "There are places where one has a simple choice between reading or madness. I was lucky enough to find a few books."

"And what makes the difference between a plebeian and a capitalist?" she asked.

Wes considered the question for a moment. "A gold mine?"

"Correct. And now, Mr. Brooks, what would a capitalist be before acquiring that gold mine?"

"I see what you're getting at."

"Do you? I sincerely doubt if you could see it unless you were stuck off in a ladies' seminary dedicated to eradicating every trace of one's hopelessly plebeian origins. Spend a few years of your life learning which corner of a visiting card to fold down. Devote an hour a day to exactly how tight one's laces must be drawn for a convincing blush and/or faint. Teach yourself not to gag at the silly prattle of show horses —unsuitable for draft or riding purposes, and perhaps you'll understand that when the money finally stopped coming and Miss Spencer oh so regretfully invited me to her office—"

"I'm sorry," Wes said. "I guess we've both come down in the world."

"Maybe *you* have, Mr. Brooks," the girl said savagely. "But *I've* finally escaped from that gaggle of empty-headed young ladies whose lives are devoted to proving their money was stolen at least two generations earlier than mine."

"My god, an anarchist!" Wes laughed. "And in his own home."

Miss Upton regained control. "Of course not. But I can't help thinking there'd be no labor troubles if they were treated better—or perhaps made privy to just how soon this mine is going to be paying no wages at all if things don't change."

"Kind of a strange attitude, isn't it?"

"Please don't misunderstand me, Mr. Brooks. My father and other men worked hard to amass capital. I have no egalitarian desire to see all that effort dissipated. I'm totally aware that no capital means no jobs at all. But if working people could see this—perhaps if our finances were open so they could see how little profit there is in this business, see how bankruptcy beckons like an easeful death—" She sighed. "But distrust feeds on itself. They'll be convinced we couldn't pay higher wages once we've closed down the mine and pay no wages at all. And when their stomachs are as empty as mine was an hour ago, will singing the 'Internationale' or 'Solidarity Forever' help fill them?"

"Man's hungry, he's not that particular about rights and wrongs."

Upton returned, buttoning a coat. "They're at it again," he said.

"Anarchists?" his daughter asked.

"Anarchists, Communists, Molly McGuires—who can keep up with them? Not a one of them with sense enough to know they're whipping a dead horse."

"What're you going to do?"

Upton shrugged. "Going back up to the headframe and make sure nobody gets into mischief." He regarded his daughter sadly. "Wish you'd stayed where I told you."

Great, Wes thought. Hired on as a stage driver and already he was being maneuvered into a private war—

maneuvered into what he instinctively suspected was the wrong side.

"You'd better stay here for a while, Mr. Brooks," the girl said. "The street could be dangerous."

Wes made a lightning evaluation of his position. The only miner with whom he'd had any personal dealings was a pick handle carrying lout by the name of—Hoggins! That was it. Someday perhaps there would be a world of peace, and perfect justice. But not in nineteen-oh-two. He had the Colt, its belt and holster rolled neatly and stacked under his hat in the front-room office. The Sharps would still be stacked in a corner of the stage depot office.

"You been having lots of trouble around here?" he asked.

"Mr. Brooks, I've been in this town about half as long as you," the girl said. "But despite a lack of firsthand knowledge . . ."

Ask a foolish question, Wes mused. "What I was wondering about was whether I ought to stay here with you or go along with himself."

"Please forgive me," she said. "I fear we're both still more tired than we realize."

"If you hate the school that much why do you still talk that way?"

Miss Upton shrugged, rearranging red hair in a way that made Wes momentarily forget his tiredness. "Habit, I suppose. The true use of speech is not so much to express our wants as to conceal them."

"Goldsmith," Wes muttered.

Miss Upton stared.

"So what are your wants?" he asked.

"A luxury which must be reserved for some other occasion, I fear. You'd better look after Father."

"And you?"

"There are arms about the house."

Wes nodded. "Good dinner," he said by way of farewell. "I'd've liked it even if I wasn't starving."

"Thank you, Mr. Brooks."

He went back out to the front office to collect his hat and Colt, but when he got there he found only his hat. For the tiniest of instants hints of unknown evils raced through his head, then he realized that, after all, the pistol was not his. Upton must have appropriated it as he left the house.

Which left the Sharps a couple of doors down the street in the stage company office. There was a spring latch on the door. He made sure it was locked behind him and faced the single dark street of Opal.

The wind had shifted and he breathed acrid smelter fumes. For a town on the verge of riot, the street did not seem all that alive. Then as his eyes adjusted to darkness he saw quiet knots of men moving uphill toward the headframe. At first he thought they had not noticed him; then as he moved downhill toward the stage office Wes noted that he was being given a wide berth.

They were all too quiet. Wes reminded himself that he was getting a hundred dollars a month, that he had risked his life for less. But there had been an implied contract then. And in the beginning he had even believed in such absurdities as Manifest Destiny. The false-fronted arch into the stage company corral had a gate across it now. He was poised to jump over it when he remembered his knee. Blast and damn!

It was as dark as a moonless night can get in a town without street lights, but there were enough eyes on him for Wes not to want to divulge how hard it was for him to climb. He studied the gate for a moment. About four feet high. If he were to take a running step and get his good left foot on the middle rail . . . He vaulted over the gate, his stiff leg flying in what an unobservant gawker might consider a flourish. The office was dark.

When he tried the door it was locked. Now where would Green Eyeshade and the company bull be? Probably up at the headframe where Wes ought to be. But his Sharps was inside and the Colt was gone. Now what the hell? No matter how this shindy turned out, his prospects for long-term employment would not be improved if he didn't turn out to show the flag.

Horses snorted and whickered in the corner of the corral. He squinted and saw the stage pushed into another corner. Then he remembered the whip.

He was in luck. Wrapping it around his waist in the darkness, he limped back toward the gate. He was considering how to get over it without calling attention to his bum leg when his fumbling hands found the latch. The gate wasn't even locked.

"Some days you just can't make a dime," he muttered. He hurried as fast as he could without limping on the uphill stretch toward the headframe. As he came closer there were the sounds of cable being winched up by a donkey engine, then the tinkle of a bell as somebody down below signaled.

The area around the hoisting machinery was lit with acetylene lamps that were brighter and flickered less than the electric lighting Wes had seen in other parts of the world. In their glow he saw a clot of miners listening to a man haranguing them from his perch atop a pile of stulls.

Wes studied the scene from the rear of the mob, trying to figure what was familiar about it. The man who was stirring up the animals wore a hat that shaded his face. He was of average height and spoke in unaccented American. Finally Wes decided that was the familiar part. He had heard these same phrases so many times in so many accents: bloodsucking capitalists, leeches, parasites on the working class, nothing to lose but your chains. He had heard the identical speech not just in English but in varying mixtures of Spanish and Tagalog. It was, like Christianity, a beautiful theory. Like Christianity, it was also totally unworkable.

But where was Upton? Where was the company bull and his men? Wes searched the crowd but saw no sign of them. He began moving around the edge of the mob, working his way toward the hoisting machine and whistle. Halfway there, he finally found Upton. The balding general manager stood quietly under the roof of the building listening to the agitator but doing nothing. As he came closer the puffy-faced company bull in the too-small derby appeared in the shadows. Upton nodded a silent greeting.

"Your property," Wes said. "You gonna let a man insult you in your own living room?"

"What would you do?" Upton asked tiredly.

Wes pondered a moment. "You did a pretty good job learning all about me," he said.

"Oh, we know who he is," the company bull said.

The orator atop the pile of stulls was warming to his subject. "Appropriate a piece of God's earth to themselves, fence out the common rabble and say, 'This is mine.' Then whose sweat brings the gold from that earth?"

"Outsider?" Wes asked.

"You don't think we'd keep him on the payroll, do you?" the company bull asked witheringly.

Wes considered the implications. Meanwhile the behatted orator was working himself into a fine frenzy over the rights of man and the injustice involved in private ownership. "Who sweats?" he demanded. "Who lives in constant danger of explosion and cave-in? Whose blood flows to fill the coffers of capitalism?"

Wes stepped clear of the hoisting-machinery shed. "Not yours," he roared in his best drill sergeant's voice. "Show me the calluses on your hands. Tell all these good people whether you've ever been underground!"

CHAPTER IX

There was a moment of shocked silence. The agitator was taken by surprise and needed nearly a second to collect himself and put down this heckler. In that second, Upton reached past the hoist engineer and grabbed the whistle cord. By the time the quilling shriek had stopped echoing, the magic moment was lost. The rapt attention of the crowd had dissolved into jeering laughter and catcalls. The man atop the pile of stulls tried again. Once more the whistle drowned him out. He tried a third time, but this time the whistle was not necessary. The "good people" of his audience were starting to throw things. As the silenced agitator clambered down from his perch amid a hail of mudballs and horsebiscuits Wes caught a momentary glimpse of a face that wavered between terror and rage.

But the mob was no longer out for blood. Laughing and joking, they began drifting back downhill. Wes found Upton and the derby-hatted company bull. "That was risky," the bull said. "What would you have done if I hadn't put a few men in there to toss the first rocks?"

Wes shrugged, feeling considerably less cocky than he had a moment ago. Upton studied him silently for a moment, then abruptly remembered: "Guess I won't be needing this." He unbuckled the Colt and handed it to Wes. He turned to the company bull and added, "Mr. Ford, could you help our friend here find some lodgings?"

They walked in silence back to the company office where

Upton unlocked and said goodnight. Wes and the company bull continued down the darkened street. "Looks like you're gonna be here a while," Ford said. "You wanna eat Bohunk or Chinese?"

"Which's best?"

Ford shrugged. "I live in the Bohunk place."

Wes guessed that was a recommendation. He followed the puffy man three doors past Yee Wing's to a boardinghouse whose door was opened by a moon-faced woman with abundant black hair tied in a tight-braided coil. Wes guessed she understood English even if she limited herself to smiles and nods while showing him a room.

There was a brass bedstead with faded coverlet, a wardrobe next to the single window. Across from the bed was a chair and a stand with a china pitcher. The basin apparently had been broken and was replaced with a tin one. Beneath the stand was a china slop jar. Wes sat on the bed and removed his boots with some difficulty. He slung them and heard one boot rebound from a thunder mug beneath the swaybacked bed. He slipped the Colt under his pillow and blew out the candle before turning in.

At first his sleep was dreamless. Then, as he had feared it might, his memory once more returned to the time he had been careless and allowed himself seriously to consider something outside himself.

There had been a red-haired woman with china-blue eyes —a woman wise in the ways of the army as only a warrant officer's daughter can be wise.

"No, Wes," she had said, sitting calmly beside a hospital bed. "I've always told you I'd never marry a sergeant. Whatever makes you think I'd marry a cripple?"

Cripple . . . nineteen years was quite a hunk out of a man's life. But the army took care of its own. Wes had always taken care of himself so far as that went. But in the company day room, filling out reports?

Someday perhaps the army would devise a weapon that could stop a *juramentado*. Wes's couldn't. He had put four slugs into the diminutive Moro and still that ninety-seven-pound soldier had split Wes's kneecap with a bolo knife before gasping, coughing blood, and calling it a lifetime.

The army took care of its own. Except when Congress went on an economy drive—except when a war turned unpopular and unwinnable, except when pacifists met troop transports at the San Francisco docks to pelt returning veterans with horse apples and rotten eggs.

Thirty-seven years old, sergeant, unblemished record. The only blemishes were on his kneecap and on his soul as he pondered the things he had done for God and country. Damn the hypocritical sons of bitches! He wasn't worth a pension. Were those congressmen worth the medals he had parcel-posted them? If the Moro had survived his *amok,* would some Sulu Sea sultan have given him a medal? Would the little man have lived to a prosperous and honored old age? At least the Moro's end had been mercifully quick, with no time to ponder the justice of his cause. But then, the little man who split Wes's kneecap had been fighting on his own ground. For God and country.

Wes woke up sweaty, the sheet in a tangle. At first he thought it was daylight, then he came fully awake with the sudden realization that he was not alone. Twice now in two days he had been caught asleep. Only thirty-seven. What had gone out of him?

There was someone sitting in the rickety chair by the window. The candle was lit again. It took him a confused moment to remember where he was. He was not used to waking up in a bed, in a room.

"To hell with it," he muttered. "Just another goddamned nightmare." But even as he said it, Wes knew it was not.

Somebody had gotten the drop on him again—just as easily as Sheriff Hurley had when he awoke in the stagecoach.

The pitcher threw an immense irregular shadow that concealed the face of the man in the chair. It did not conceal the glint of a steel gun barrel that pointed at Wes. "Just keep your hands in sight," the visitor cautioned.

Under the circumstances Wes decided there was little else he could do. Damn it! If he hadn't been so bone tired, he'd've checked out this room better. There was a hook and eye on the door. Still hooked. His visitor had come in through the second-story window. Wes wondered if there was a porch roof outside or if he had used a ladder. As if it made any difference!

Then as he came fully awake Wes realized that, though browning around the edges, his goose was by no means cooked as yet. If the visitor had wanted to kill him he could have done it while Wes slept. "Where is it?" the stranger asked.

"Oh hell!" Wes growled. "That again?"

"That again."

It had to be one of the also-rans of this afternoon's encounter when he had shot one yellow-haired bandit and Miss Upton had laid open the face of another. "Tell you what I'm gonna do," Wes said conversationally, "if you blow out the candle before you leave, I'll go back to sleep."

"And if I don't?"

"Must be a dozen rooms in this place and the walls aren't that thick," Wes said. "Chances are men're waking up and getting ready to complain already. If I 'uz t'give a couple of war whoops . . ."

"You SOB, I been waitin' for a chance to use this!" The man in the shadows waved the pistol menacingly.

"You'll never get a better chance."

"I'm warnin' you!"

Wes laughed. "I know you are. But you're more interested in knowing where it is. Otherwise I wouldn't've woke up now, would I?"

There was a moment of silence as the man in the shadows squirmed and shifted his pistol to his other hand. Then he came toward the bed. In his right hand was an Arkansas toothpick. Wes studied the thin, stilettolike blade and wished he'd been able to wake up with his hand under the pillow—or the Colt somewhere closer to reach.

As his visitor stepped forward his face came out of the shadow and Wes's suspicions were verified. He had seen that face somewhere before. A lot of good it was going to do him. His throat was dry with tension. He swallowed and moved his tongue. The movement was not lost on the man with the gun and the Arkansas toothpick. "Ready to change your tune?" he asked, bending over the bed.

Wes's mouth worked, but he did not speak. Grinning, the gunman bent lower over his supine form. Flat on his back, Wes thought. Of all the damned ways to be caught. His mouth moved again, but nothing came out.

"Cat gotcher tongue?" the stranger gloated. He began moving the tip of the Arkansas toothpick with tantalizing slowness toward Wes's crotch.

"YAAAAAAAAAH!" Wes emitted an explosive shriek and a gob of spittle. The stranger's eyes widened and his hands went slack for the briefest of instants. Wes's fist did not.

The gun went off deafeningly and beneath the bed Wes heard the tinkle of china as the thunder mug shattered. The Arkansas toothpick dug into the mattress beside him as he got an arm around the stranger's neck and pulled him down. They grappled briefly, but the fight was over before it started, the stranger still not quite realizing what had hit him when Wes gave him a final whack alongside the head with the heavy butt of the Arkansas toothpick. He was fully dressed and pulling his boots on when the first excited knocking came at his door.

It was Ford. Wes wondered momentarily how the company bull had gotten here so quickly, then remembered Ford lived in this same boardinghouse. "I got a feeling this's one of your stage robbers," Wes said. "Sure wish I knew why he's houndin' me."

Ford turned the unconscious stranger over and studied his pale face. "Looks abused," he said. "I hope you ain't goin' to turn out this noisy every night."

Wes hoped so too. "Got a place to hold him?"

The company bull nodded, prodding the stranger into consciousness with the toe of his boot. At gunpoint he encouraged Wes's visitor down the hall through a half-clothed mob of the curious and the half-asleep. As Ford and his captive disappeared downstairs the miners turned to Wes. "Ain't you the new stage driver?" one asked.

"Ain't you the feller give Hoggins his comeuppance?"

"Sorry," Wes said, and shook his head. "It's long past bedtime." He closed his door and hooked it before going to study the open window. There was no ladder. Handy beneath his window was a shed roof that made ladders unnecessary for anyone with enough gumption to stand on a rain barrel and shinny up a short length of drainpipe.

Tomorrow he was going to have to inspect this house and see if there was such a thing as a secure room. On that thought he went back to bed.

But Wes had slept just enough, had just enough excitement that sleep was not to be so easily seduced a second time. He lay facing the ceiling, listening to the periodic creak and chuff of the hoisting engine. This time of night there was not so much noise in the streets, and when the wind was right he could even hear the jingle of signal bells. Somewhere in the distance, there was a shout, then a single shot. A dog yipped once.

He dozed and was awakened by the pressure wave and faint earthquakelike shudder of a blast. Wes had been around dynamite enough to know the soul-shattering headache that could result from breathing the fumes. Was this mine well ventilated? He didn't know all that much about mining, but it seemed to him that usually a shot was fired at the end of a shift, then the place was left several hours for smoke and dust to clear before the next shift went underground. Yet here at the Opal mine blasting seemed to go off any time of day or night.

He was still awake when a whistle blew with that prolonged, marrow-melting shriek that could rouse the deepest of sleepers. He lay rigid, gritting his teeth and waiting for it to stop. It didn't.

How many hours was the damned thing going to keep blowing? There was no hope of getting any more sleep now. He might as well get up. Though it was probably not more than thirty seconds, it seemed to Wes that the whistle had been keening for as many hours.

He stared red-eyed out the window at a faint grayness in the eastern sky. He sighed and began picking up the clothes he had scattered over the floor. Was the damned whistle stuck? Had the cord broken or been cut by some malcontent? It was still keening away, gouging shreds from his sanity like Philippine joy or Irish woe.

He knelt and fumbled amid shards of the chamber pot for his other boot, wondering annoyedly at the clumping rumble of other boots down the hallway.

And only then did he begin to suspect what was wrong. Wes stuck his head out the window and knew he was not going to have a quiet stroll by himself. Every man in town and half the women were running uphill toward the headframe. They were all miners. They all knew what the shriek of a nonstop whistle meant.

CHAPTER X

Wes had not been that much around mines, but he had heard of the way everyone in town turned out in an emergency. Made sense, he supposed. The company too would stint nothing in its efforts to save whoever was trapped if ever they hoped to lure men underground again. He supposed he ought to get up there to the mine and do what he could to help. But he was damned if he knew what.

He finished pulling his boots on, buckled the Colt, remembered the whip as he was leaving the room. There were times he felt like an idiot with all this stuff hung on and about him—but not half as silly as he'd felt on the odd occasion when he didn't have his equipment. Everybody else was charging up Opal's single street toward the headframe and that marrow-melting whistle. Wes went with them as far as the company office. He reached the door just as Upton was coming out. "Name it," Wes said.

Upton gave him the confused look of a man not quite awake, then recognized him. "Yes," he hmmmed. "Better go see how bad it is first."

They trudged on together toward the headframe. Upton last night had been a balding, middle-aged man beset with worries. In the dawn's early light he was positively cadaverous. "Something wrong?" Wes asked.

Upton gave him an odd look.

"I mean apart from this."

"You mean apart from disappearing profits, labor troubles, stage robberies, and now a cave-in?"

Wes decided it would be undiplomatic to ask the harried manager if he looked this poorly every morning. They reached the headframe and pushed through the knot of people crowding around a dirty man whose carbide head lamp was still burning.

"It's in the new section," the headlit man said when he saw Upton. "Must be a dozen men trapped. Twelfth level."

Abruptly Upton was even older and more tired. He and the man with the head lamp went into the engineering shack beside the headframe and Wes followed. The talk grew recondite. Wes thought he knew what a shaft was and he could guess at tunnels, galleries, and chutes. But what was the difference between a drift, a winze, and a stope? They pulled great sheets of paper from a vertical file where drawings hung by their edges and spread them about the office, and gradually Wes discovered that he hadn't even known what a shaft was. Instead of descending vertically into the earth, shafts followed the vein in this country where, thanks to some prehistoric catastrophe, every stratum tilted fifty-two degrees.

A drift, he finally decided, was a horizontal tunnel following the vein away from the shaft. If it went up or down, it became a winze. While Upton and the other man who had still not remembered to extinguish his lamp nattered on, Wes surveyed the engineering office with its drafting table and files, its shelf of books along one wall. He picked one and discovered that a stope is a stair-stepped work face to give men a foothold while digging. Were gold and silver veins thick enough for stoping? Apparently they were at Opal.

Outside, the few women of the town had improvised a field kitchen and were boiling coffee. As he watched, Miss

Upton and Tinacling arrived bearing sacks of provisions. And Wes was doing nothing. . . . Upton and the other man seemed to have forgotten him as they pored over drawings, scheming how to get around a cave-in and dig out the trapped miners. Wes stepped out of the office.

The signal bells had been tinkling constantly as the cage went up and down taking fresh relays of men below. Wes stood on the edge of the crowd trying to make some sense of this organized chaos when somebody nudged him. It was Hoggins, the bull-man who had menaced him with a pick handle. "Ye know how to fight well enow," the swollen-nosed mucker growled, and for the first time West realized he was a Cousin Jack. "But do you know haow to dig?"

It seemed like a fair question. "I got two hands," Wes said. And a moment later he found himself in the cage, crowded in with eleven dirty men on his first trip under-ground. The Cornishman whose nose he had flattened was one of his fellow passengers as a bell jangled and the cage dropped with a stomach-loosening jerk, grinding and rat-tling down a fifty-two-degree slope. Wes tried not to think what would happen if that slender steel cable above his head were to break.

The top of the cage was open, with nothing to break the fall of whatever were to come tumbling down upon them. Surely it wouldn't cost all that much to put a grating up there. . . . But if his fellow passengers were concerned, they didn't show it. Despite a dusty coating of black grease the pulley was shrieking like a priest in a Protestant hell as the cable ran through it. He remembered the size of the drum on that hoisting machine and wondered how much had been paid out already.

It seemed to him that they had been dropping forever into the darkness that rushed by so fast he could distinguish nothing of the shaft face. Then, finally, the sickening drop slowed and his knees bowed. A moment later men were jumping the yard-wide gap from cage to a tunnel floor.

Somehow his hat had disappeared, replaced by a peaked cap with a sewn-in bracket for a carbide lamp. Wes was familiar with the lamp, having used them often enough in remote outposts.

What he was not familiar with was being underground, with full knowledge that there was earth above him—loose earth, rocks that could at any moment come crashing down and solve all his problems permanently. He had faced danger many times, but never this kind. He studied the stolid Cousin Jack faces around him and reminded himself that he had once been a sergeant.

He followed them through what he supposed was a gallery, an immense chamber whose roof was supported by wood and stone cribbing. Unrelenting pressure from above had compressed the foot-thick wooden balks into less than half their original thickness without splitting them. He glanced up and quartz glinted in the light of his lamp. Then, as they passed exhausted men coming out, there was abruptly no overhead reflection from his light. A moment later they came to the spot where loose rocks and rubble covered the tracks of the miniature railroad. He joined the others in struggling to dig out a half-buried car.

An hour later the car had been extricated and pushed to the shaft where it was dumped and brought back for a fresh load. Wes's leg was bothering him, but at least the cave-in had given the miners full headroom to work standing up. He was swinging his pick at the rockfall when Hoggins thrust mouth to ear and said, "Ee'v done. Stand back and let a fresh lad in."

Wes was tired enough and more than eager to see the sun and surface again. But precisely because he was so frightened of this totally alien environment he made himself hang back and walk as casually as if this were another drill field. By the time he reached the cage, it was full to capacity. He moved back a ways in the drift and found a place to sit. Damn, how his leg was hurting!

So he had been wrong about Hoggins. The bull-man had borne no grudge. If he had, there would have been plenty of opportunities underground where Wes was at as much of a disadvantage as the Cousin Jack had been above. He considered the hour he had spent digging here. This, he supposed, was the twelfth level. The shaft continued downward, so it could not be the bottom of the mine.

There were Sherlock Holmes types of men who could take a single glance at something totally unfamiliar and immediately see relationships never fathomed by those who spent their lives there. Wes was not one of them. He had briefly glimpsed the mine's general plan up in the engineering office. Where in hell was he? Bells jangled and an ore bucket came down the shaft, a man holding the cable and standing on the bail. Wes could go up with the load of rock they were dumping into this car. Could—but had no intention of so doing. Without knowing where or when to jump off he could end up on the tailings dump buried beneath that rock—or perhaps inside the rock crusher.

Two men tipped the handcar into the ore bucket and pushed it back to the face again. The bucket moved up the shaft, leaving Wes sitting in relative quiet. At that moment his lamp chose to go out.

The darkness was total. He fought down rising panic, knowing he was in no real danger. In a moment, somebody would come along and he could borrow a handful of carbide. As for water, it wouldn't be the first time he had peed into a carbide lamp. He unhooked it from his cap and began taking it apart to shake out the sludge.

He remembered reading a story once about a lost miner

who had listened to the earth groan as it moved—a story of a man who had listened too long to ghosts and finally begun answering them. Here, with the constant jangle of bells, the muffled sounds of men working a hundred yards away at the face of the cave-in, the banshee shriek of cable and pulleys, there was slight chance of overhearing anything so subtle as any earth movement. He wondered if the men trapped had gotten the slightest inkling of anything amiss in the moments before the roof had fallen in on them.

God damn it! The brass cupful of sludge slipped from his fingers and went rattling around on the floor of the drift. If he didn't find it before somebody came along with a light he would be branded for the incompetent he was. Taking his Creator's name in vain, he performed his stiff-kneed courtier's bow and began scrabbling blindly, hunting for the bottom half of his lamp.

Where was the motherless thing? Surely it couldn't have jumped over the rail. Had to be somewhere on this side of the tunnel. He tried to remember his directions. Already he was totally turned around. If he didn't watch it he was going to go tumbling down the shaft. Watch it . . . his straining eyes saw nothing but gray-flecked blackness. Moving carefully, he crawled and felt his way hunting for the carbide cup. He felt the rail and reversed to head away from it.

Still feeling his way to avoid the bottomless pit of the shaft, he scrabbled around until he felt a solid rock face. But which way was the shaft? Ought to sit still and wait for somebody to come along. But he was damned if he was going to be caught helpless, on his knees in the dark. Find that damned cup, find his seat again, regain his composure, and do his best not to make a fool of himself.

And still he couldn't find the accursed thing. A sergeant was not expected to make unseemly displays, so he gritted his teeth and refrained from tracing the ancestry of whoever invented carbide lamps. Why couldn't they have a length of chain or somesuch to keep the parts together?

A bell jangled and pulleys began to shriek. Damn! They were going to find him on his knees fumbling around in the dark! He cupped hands behind his ears and rotated his head, trying to decide which way the hoisting machinery and shaft were. There were too many echoes for him to be sure. Noise came from everywhere.

The rattle and roar of the hoist became louder, peaked, and began lessening. Must have been an ore bucket because it went on past without the slightest flicker of light. It was the first he knew that even now the mine was still working. Or was it? Maybe men were tunneling up from a different level. Either way he was still alone in the darkness, still on his knees feeling his way about as he hunted for the bottom of that illegitimate lamp.

His stiff leg struck something. He felt and it was the rail again. Was his time sense distorted? It seemed as if he had been hours here alone in the darkness, and yet he knew that now that they had freed an ore car to move the muck away from the face the hurrying men had been filling one every ten minutes.

Reason told him to give up. Sit and rest and sooner or later somebody would be along. It wasn't as if he'd been stupid enough to wander off into some unused part of the mine where he might wait forever. But losing one's lamp in the darkness, he suspected, must be roughly equivalent to dropping one's rifle on the parade ground. Nobody might say anything to him, but Wes knew what would be said behind his back, what everyone would think every time he showed his face in Opal. With a bad knee he had one too many handicaps now. He had to find that goddamned lamp.

The pulley shriek crescendoed as the ore bucket came back up the shaft, but this time it stopped briefly. Still in a darkness as black as his dreams, the hoist started again.

Somebody, he suspected, had rung the wrong signal. Or maybe the overworked hoist engineer had made a mistake. The bucket creaked and shrieked away and still he was on his one good knee fumbling for that lamp cup. He must have gotten turned around and headed in a totally wrong direction.

There was only one thing to do. He remembered about how far he had been sitting from the shaft. He would have to crawl until he felt the nothingness where drift met shaft, then he would know where he was, could feel his way back and zigzag until he found that aniparous lamp bottom. He barked his shin on the rail again and managed not to remark upon it.

Run his hand along the rail. Go fifty feet or so, and if the rail didn't end, he was heading back toward the cave-in instead of the shaft. He did and in less than a foot his hand found the block that was part of the dumping mechanism at the shaft end of the line. He had been crawling around within inches of disaster.

Where was that *yen shee* baby of a lamp cup? He turned around and began feeling his zigzag way back toward where he had lost it. And finally, after all this fiddling around he had an idea.

He had lost the bottom of the lamp, but he hadn't lost the top. The lamp had a flint and wheel to spark it alight. Without a bottom the lamp wouldn't light, but he could strike a spark. By now his eyes should be so open that a spark would be as good as daylight.

He spun the wheel and it sparked. It wasn't exactly daylight, but it was enough to see by. He didn't see the bottom of his lamp. Instead, he saw a man facing him in the darkness less than a yard away. Wes wondered if he was as startled as the other man seemed. But now he was once more in darkness.

CHAPTER XI

Wes was so startled he nearly dropped the rest of the useless lamp. He drew a deep breath and spun the wheel again. This time the man was gone. He saw the bottom of his lamp a foot or two behind where the apparition had been and moved to grab it before he could become disoriented again.

And just in time. An ore car was rumbling down the track and an instant later he saw the headlights of the two men pushing it. He was going to ask them for carbide, and he was going to ask what another man was doing poking around in the darkness. Then, finally, a fresh carload of muckers stopped at the twelfth level and he was riding up in the empty car with an aged tobacco chewer. It was too noisy to talk, and by the time he reached the surface he had forgotten about it.

"Well, Mr. Brooks. I didn't know you were a miner too." It was Miss Upton who handed him a heavy mug of coffee and a cheese sandwich.

"I'm not," he said. "I dug a while, but I still don't know what's going on down there."

"Neither, apparently, does anyone else," Miss Upton sighed. "But by now at least they've swept out the saloons and found three of the missing men."

"How many does that leave?"

"Nine."

Wes sipped coffee and wolfed the sandwich, abruptly realizing that he'd missed breakfast again. The girl handed

him another. "Anything else I can do?" he asked when he
had finished.

"You might go take a bath," the girl suggested with a
hint of amusement.

He was, Wes abruptly realized, as thoroughly mudded up
as all the other men coming out of the cage. They descended on the women's free lunch counter and Wes moved
on. He'd done his bit down below. Upton was nowhere in
sight, nor did he see hide nor hair of the company bull. He
supposed the Indian boy was off scouting more bread or
coffee or whatever for the ladies' auxiliary. Feeling tired
and useless, Wes moseyed down the single street to his
boardinghouse. As he had expected, there was no one there.
Like every other woman in town, his landlady was probably
up at the pithead feeding the men.

He checked the pitcher and it was half empty. He poured
what there was in the basin and went downstairs looking for
a well. There was none, but there were two barrels of water
in the kitchen. He refilled the pitcher and went back upstairs through the empty house to perform his ablutions.

It was not even noon yet. He was sleepy after a busy
night but knew a nap now would only mean another sleep-
less night. Then, alone at last, he knew what he ought to be
doing. He went into the back yard and picked through the
landlady's trash heap for bottles. Two rounds with the Colt
and he knew he needn't waste more time getting ac-
quainted. He unlimbered the whip and spent an hour getting the hang of snapping the necks off bottles without
knocking them over.

There was something wrong. There were a lot of things
wrong, but Wes was not troubled about the obvious things.
What bothered him was—good luck for a change. Why was
he so lucky? Things had gone so sour for so long that he
had stopped trying to please anyone. Despite his crusty

manner, he had gotten a job driving the stage back down to
the county seat. And once there he had been snappish with
Polk, only to have that irate little man suddenly turn amia-
ble and offer him a job for twice what it was worth. Men
were driving stages every day for less than a hundred dollars a month, he suspected. Why was he getting all this
lovely money for a once-a-week run? What was it got him
smiles and dinner from a mine owner's daughter? Wes was
thirty-seven, had a bad knee and not a dime to his name. He
was not ugly, but he had never considered himself hand-
some either. What was the secret of his sudden charm? He
sighed and returned to his room via the back door of the
empty boardinghouse.

Going to have to do something about that room. He had
a key, but anybody could shinny up that drainpipe and in
his window. Somebody already had. Damn, was he ever
tired! An hour of swinging a pick underground had taken
more out of him than it should. Grudgingly, he pulled off
his boots and slung them under the bed. Now what was
that?

He remembered a few hours ago when an also-ran's bullet had perforated his mattress and shattered the thunder
mug. He looked under the bed where he had slung his boots
and sure enough, the landlady had been goldbricking. The
shards of shattered thunder mug were still there. Then he
realized it wasn't really her fault. Poor woman had been
called out at dawn just as he had been by the cave-in. She
hadn't had time yet to swamp out these rooms.

But gold brick or not, there was something under Wes's
bed that he was sure the landlady didn't know about. He
grasped it and tugged. Heavy. But after all, this was a real
gold brick and not the army kind. It was made out of
real gold.

He hefted it. There must be five pounds of gold in

this ingot. Even in his new hundred-dollar-a-month magnificence this was worth nearly two years' pay. Of all the nice things that had happened to him lately, this was the one that decided Wes. It was too good to be true. Entirely too good.

Somebody had been laying some complex and careful plans for Wes. Plans that had gone astray only because a landlady had been interrupted by a cave-in whistle and hadn't gotten around to cleaning up his room.

There were several things Wes could do. He considered the simplest and most obvious: Take the money and run. He wondered if he'd make it halfway to the bottom of Opal's single street. Was anybody watching now? From the corner of his eye he studied the window. The blind was up, but the going-ragged curtain covered the lower half. He sat on the bed with a gold ingot in his lap and tried to figure what to do with it. Then abruptly he knew where to put it—where to hide it right in this same house. It was going to be interesting to see what happened next.

Up by the headframe it was business as usual. He sat on his bed listening to the jangle of bells, the chuff and scree of the hoisting machinery. From the window he could see most of Opal's single street. It was slowly returning to normal as men finished their stint at the cave-in and drifted home to rest. Wes did what had to be done before somebody else returned to the boardinghouse. Then he went out onto the street. Was he only imagining it or did people seem friendlier now that he'd taken his turn underground?

At loose ends, he went into the stage company corral to see if anyone had remembered the horses. He still didn't know who swamped out around here. Tinacling? The Indian boy seemed to be the principal dog robber in this town.

The stage office was empty, but the horses had water and oats. They greeted him with the unqualified love of exploited for exploiter. He stood at the fence patting their muzzles and talking nonsense, thinking dark thoughts of draft horses and draft men and how at last their faith brought both to the glue factory.

And then that marrow-melting whistle began again. At first Wes thought it was another cave-in, then the shrieking broke into a series of joyous yips. In the silence after the whistle ceased, he could hear over the sound of machinery a groundswell of human voices cheering. So the trapped men had been dug out . . . how many of them still alive?

"Ah, Mr. Brooks." Wes turned and it was Ford, the company bull in the too-small derby. His puffy face was wreathed in smiles.

Wes nodded, despising himself for a thread of suspicion. Suspicion was the company bull's business, not his. It was a joyous occasion, rescued miners and all. Why shouldn't Ford be smiling?

The man in the too-small derby glanced around the deserted corral. He put his fingers to lips. Wes wondered if he thought the horses would carry tales. "Some odd things've been happening around here lately," he said in a low voice.

This struck Wes as the biggest understatement since the government had admitted that all was not well in the Philippines.

"Few of us're having a little meetin'. Might be a good idea if you sat in."

To Wes it sounded like an invitation to a poker game. He followed Ford out of the stage company corral and back across the street to the Bohunk boardinghouse. As they came near, Tinacling appeared, trotting up toward the headframe with still another load of groceries. He gave them a hurried nod, and as he passed Wes noted a surreptitious gesture from one brown hand. He wondered if Ford had seen it.

Probably not. Ford was too busy skinning his teeth and raising his too-small derby to somebody else. Wes turned and saw Upton heading toward them, still looking like warmed-over death despite the good news from the mine. Is he in on it? Wes wondered. Or was this whole show for Upton's benefit? In silence the trio climbed the stairs of the empty boardinghouse.

"Your room," Ford suggested, "where we can watch the street."

Wes shrugged and tried to appear unsuspecting as he unlocked the door. He sat on the bed. Upton took the single chair and Ford stood by the door. Nobody spoke. Finally Wes realized they were waiting for somebody else. Moments later he heard steps and a discreet tap on the door. Ford opened it and the green-eyeshaded station agent came in, grinning nervously. Despite their choice of his room, nobody seemed particularly interested in the street.

Ford's eyes kept straying to the bed where Wes sat. Wes had had his doubts all along. Now he knew who sat where and how the sides in this game were chosen up. "By the way," he asked, suddenly remembering that single shot in the darkness, "how's that scoundrel we caught in here last night doing? He have any information?"

"Dead," Ford said shortly. "Damn fool took it in his head to make a run for it right in the middle of the street."

Somehow the news didn't surprise Wes as much as it should have. "Too bad you couldn't have questioned him first," he said. "Be nice to know what in hell's going on around here."

"Oh," Green Eyeshade said with a nervous giggle, "we're startin' to get a pretty good idea about that."

I just bet you are, Wes thought. Green Eyeshade and Ford were both unable to conceal their interest in his bed, or what lay under it. Wes caught Upton's quiet observing eye and then he knew the manager and principal stock-holder was also part of this charade.

Or was he? Upton had mentioned disappearing profits as if they were a thing apart from stage robberies. Wes began to suspect they were. Labor troubles . . . even socialists—their leaders anyway—could understand a balance sheet. There was no point in stirring up trouble at a mine that was ready to go broke. "So somebody's got his hand in the till?" Wes asked. "Maybe layin' it all onto a bunch of bandits when they're only gettin' the leavin's?" He paused a minute and added, "That'd explain why perfect strangers keep askin' me *'Where is it?'* I s'pose a man'd feel pretty put out to hear he got away with a lot when he didn't get anything but small change."

Upton sat silent in the only chair, his eyes not leaving Wes. Green Eyeshade and Ford were getting jumpier, eyes darting continually to the space beneath his bed. "For a stranger you got it figured out pretty fast," Ford said, pushing his too-small derby back from his porcine face. "Only trouble is, it ain't quite that way."

Suddenly Wes knew he had been wrong on one important point. But he had worked it out about thirty seconds too late. What difference did it make how much gold they planted in his room now? He studied Upton's watchful face and wondered if that silent and watchful man had figured it out too.

"Gold started disappearing just about the time you turned up in this country," Green Eyeshade said with that tic that was half cough, half giggle.

Now that, Wes knew, was just plain not true. The stage had been being robbed for months—while he'd been on the high seas, aboard a troop transport returning from Manila, and with four thousand witnesses. He wondered if Upton knew it too. Of course he did. He'd told Wes he'd looked pretty carefully into every stranger's past. Too bad the balding man hadn't looked closer to home. Green Eyeshade moved unobtrusively behind Upton's chair. Did either of these two eager bunglers realize how much Upton knew about "the stranger in town"?

"Could I see your pistol a minute?" Ford said.

"The company's pistol," Wes corrected. "The gun that passed through God only knows how many hands before I first laid eyes on it a couple of days ago. The gun that Mr. Upton borrowed last night, for example." Suddenly he was tired of all this pussyfooting around. "You might as well have a look under the bed, too," he said tiredly. "Not that you're going to find much apart from a busted thunder mug."

"Your pistol," Ford repeated. "Just hand it over now slow and easy." The company bull was pointing a Smith and Wesson hammerless at Wes.

Wes shrugged. "You ain't gonna lay it on me," he said, and handed over the pistol. Turning to Upton, he added, "I ain't the kind to commit suicide and I ain't crazy enough to try to run from a man's got a gun on me. You keep that in mind if these two jimdandies try'n tell you I ran." He glared at Upton, struggling to put across the urgent message behind his bluster.

Upton shook his head. "I've had my head in the sand long enough," he said. Looking at Ford and the stage depot manager, he added, "There's little doubt now who the scoundrels are."

Wes held his breath, knowing it was too late now. Leisurely, the man in the too-small derby hat shot Mr. Upton. With Wes's Colt.

CHAPTER XII

Upton gave a look of vague surprise and fell sideways out of the chair. "And now you," Green Eyeshade said with that nervous cough-giggle. But Ford shook his head. "He's right," he said, pointing at Wes with the still-smoking Colt. "Looks funny if too many men die resisting arrest. Besides, we got him. Did it with the gun he's been wearin' all over town. Ain't nobody gonna give a damn whether it's his or the company's."

From the floor the balding Upton gave a final rattling sigh and bloody phlegm appeared around his mouth. Green Eyeshade gave that nervous giggle again. Ford glanced at the man he had shot with as much passion as if he'd been a squashed cockroach. With the Colt, he motioned Wes to his feet.

Wes arose cautiously, knowing the company bull would like to tie up loose ends, but that he was not indispensable. Anybody who had been robbing Upton and the mine blind this long, playing bandits and sheriff against one another—this puffy-faced man with the too-small derby didn't really need Wes.

In a way Wes was almost relieved. Since he had accepted five dollars to drive that stage down to Okapogum he had known something was wrong. Men's luck didn't change like that. Men made their own luck. And by accepting too much money, by believing the bitch goddess of success might this once have filed the barbs from her harpoon, he had made his own luck. He felt a curious sense of relief as he marched down the hall and across the street at pistol point. Now things were back to normal.

Half the town seemed to be on the streets watching his fall from grace. The other half would know about it within minutes. And Miss Upton. . . Wes felt a pang at the realization that if ever he were to see that capable young lady again, chances were she would be the one to whip the horses from beneath him.

Opal's hoosegow was half dug into the solid rock of the mountainside at the upper end of town, toward the mine. The room above ground was of tapered rock-and-mortar walls that gave the place an upward flare like a cup. High above him was a roof of heavy beams and corrugated iron. Wes sat in a corner of the cool, damp room and meditated on his shortcomings.

This room, he guessed, had not been intended as a jail. But it would do until a proper jail came along. The lower walls were nearly a yard thick. The door was of iron-sheathed-and-banded oak with hinges clear across it and a hasp on the outside. He studied the tapering walls and chalice shape. Despite the heaviness of the walls, the roof was not all that massive.

Wes had seen rooms like this before. Shaped like a mortar, heavy at the bottom and lighter at the top. He was in a powder magazine. Abandoned now, but originally this rocky chamber had been built to divert an explosion harmlessly outward and upward. Blow the roof off and save the town. He wondered where the Opal Mining and Development Company kept its dynamite nowadays. But mostly, he wondered if there were any possible way to get out of this place.

Not that it could do him all that much good. Where could he go? The only way out of this country was down through the county seat—bottled up by the sheriff even if he could get a horse. Up farther in the hills from Opal. . . . Only bears and Indians knew what was up in those mountains apart from the summer-long snow.

But there had to be refuge somewhere. How did stagecoach robbers survive? He had a sneaking suspicion that they survived incognito and very comfortably either in Okapogum or in Opal. That would never work for Wes whose face was too well known, whose limp made him stand out a mile away. But why worry about that? The longest journey begins with a step, but the first step of any escape had to be outside an iron-banded oaken door with broad hinges and a mining company padlock on a hasp. He studied the straw tick in the corner and guessed it would be no worse than the floor.

If only he'd worked it out a split second sooner. . . . Should have realized from the beginning which side Upton was on. He could have saved that man's life. If only Upton hadn't shot off his mouth . . . if he'd just gone along with it, pretended he believed Wes guilty, they could have gotten out of that room, could have bagged Ford and Green Eyeshade at their leisure. Now Upton was dead.

Wes might as well be dead himself. They would lay Upton's murder onto him. And in a way he was guilty. He lay down and closed his eyes, realizing that at last his run of bad luck had come to an end. They couldn't do anything more to him now.

Poor Miss Upton . . . barely home in time to bury her father. Perhaps she would feel better after Wes was hung. She didn't seem the sort who would be inclined toward any softheaded forgiveness for murderers. Miss Upton was too smart for that. Miss Upton was a very intelligent girl.

And suddenly Wes realized they had still not done everything to him that they might. Miss Upton was alive. As long as she believed Wes guilty of her father's murder she would stay alive. If she ever showed the slightest doubt she would be dead too.

Green Eyeshade and Ford must own a few shares. Somehow they would euchre the girl out of her controlling interest. And if she refused to be maneuvered . . . He had to get out of here!

He studied the sloping walls. The rock was rough and a skillful climber with two good legs might make it to the roof. But, though a small dynamite explosion could lift the roof off easily, there wasn't that much dynamite left in Wes. He lay staring up at the roof, thinking of horses, of guns, of all the things he would need if ever he were to figure a way to get out of here.

An hour passed and there was no way. From here he could see the roof was more than bare hands could rip apart even if he were to devise some stiff-legged way of climbing the eighteen or twenty feet up the rock and mortar wall. From the footprints that marred the whitewash he could see that better men—two-legged men—had already explored that possibility.

He ought to be scheming frantically, but he was overcome with the lethargy of total defeat. They would kill him. If he were by some miracle to communicate with the girl and convince her of his innocence, he would only manage to get her killed too.

She had been decent about not exposing his ignorance of horses. She had treated him like a human being, fed him, and had not simpered over him like some silly schoolgirl. The least he could do, Wes decided, was keep his mouth shut and save her life.

There was the sound of key in padlock and the door opened. Gun in hand, Ford poked his puffy face into the gloom. Reassured by the sight of Wes supine on the straw tick in the far corner, he put a willow basket on the floor and kicked it toward him. Wordlessly, the company bull backed out of the powder magazine and locked the door again.

Wes got stiffly to his feet and recovered the basket. Instead of the usual tablecloth cover of a picnic basket, this one had brown wrapping paper. He opened it and discovered what must once have been a well-prepared meal. But that would have been before Ford broke every biscuit apart —as if anybody could conceal a hacksaw blade in a biscuit. The venison steak was cold but edible. Even that had been clumsily quartered with a dull knife. A mound of mashed potatoes and gravy had long since congealed, but the dull knife had stirred them up too.

It was just silly, small-minded meanness. Wes ate cautiously, afraid Ford might have planned something amusing with pepper and salt, but though the meal was cold and poked over, it was almost as delicious as the last time he had eaten venison steak at—at Upton's office-home, cooked by the dead man's capable daughter.

No wonder Ford had been cautious. For a queasy instant Wes thought of tasteless poisons, then he knew the capable Miss Upton would not do it that way. If she believed what Ford and Green Eyeshade had told her about her father's death, that young lady would wait for due process at the end of a state-authorized rope.

In spite of being half in the rock, this improvised jail was also half out of the rock and, unventilated, it was getting uncomfortably warm in here. The girl—was she the only cook in town? Why, he wondered, had Ford accepted a meal prepared by her?

It had to be. He recognized the wheat-sheaf pattern of the heavy sterling knife and fork. Same stuff he had eaten with at the Upton home that night so long ago. So long ago . . .

it had only been night before last! Why sterling silverware in jail?

As if she had known it would be hot in here, there was no coffee with the meal. He pulled the cork from what had once been a whiskey bottle and sniffed. Lemonade. He took a drink and nearly strangled. It wasn't lemonade. It was pure lemon juice without a drop of sugar. Must have cost the better part of a dollar to get that many lemons this far north.

An expensive prank. He would never have believed Miss Upton capable of such small-mindedness. He sighed and waited for the strangling sourness to leave his mouth. Finally he could finish the venison, the mashed potatoes, the biscuits. Eat, drink, and be merry, he thought. But something was bothering him.

Why had the girl sent him a meal? Hadn't he just "murdered" her father? He sat on the straw tick and considered the remains of the brown paper wrapped lunch. Had she been trying to tell him something? It must have been all neatly wrapped and prepared until Ford had had to go poking through it all. He wiped grease from his hands and mouth and discovered that, though the girl had not included a napkin, she had put several toothpicks in with the meal.

It was anybody's guess what was going through her mind. Probably, distraught with grief, she hadn't been thinking clearly about anything. There were practical considerations too. To the best of his knowledge there was no ice in this town. Nor did Opal boast an undertaker who might know something of embalming. The weather was warm. Wes remembered the indecent haste with which burials had taken place in the sweltering Philippines. Chances were Miss Upton was seeing her father go underground at this moment. It would not do to wait another day.

So she had given him unsweetened lemon juice instead of

lemonade. If that were the worst she did on the day she buried a murdered father the world had no cause to label her flighty. All things considered, she had performed wonders with the stringy, slightly overage venison. He picked shreds of meat from his teeth and released a genteel belch. *The condemned man ate a hearty meal . . .*

It would have been more like Ford to bring him slops from the Bohunk boardinghouse—or from Yee Wing's down the street. The only possible solution that occurred to Wes was that the girl might have prepared immense quantities of food for the cave-in and there was no point in letting it go to waste.

That had to be it. It was only an accident that he had happened upon something prepared by the girl's own hands, had fed himself with that same wheat-sheaf-adorned silverware. Probably she didn't even know her food had been abstracted from the rescue workers' free lunch to feed the man who had murdered her father.

He was raising the bottle to his mouth when he remembered it was unadulterated lemon juice. Maybe he was supposed to use it to take away the rusty iron taste from the bucket and dipper in the corner of the powder magazine.

Damn this jail! Less than two hours ago he had sponged off the mud and grit of the Opal mine and already he felt gritty, could feel the itching precursor of what promised to be full-scale torment once it turned dark and the straw tick's natives became restless.

He sat dispiritedly, hoping it was the way he had worked it out—that it was only an accident that he had ended up with the girl's box lunch at this perverted social. If she were careless enough to try to communicate with him . . .

He had almost convinced himself of this comforting illusion when Wes remembered how carefully his lunch had been picked over. Ford wouldn't bother if he had picked food at random. Ford knew who had prepared this meal. Ford suspected.

The girl was committing suicide just as her father had. And there was nothing he could do to warn her. Wes wiped his suddenly sweaty brow with the brown paper. Why hadn't she stuck in a napkin or at least a rag? Then abruptly he saw the full depths of Miss Upton's duplicity. She had fooled Ford. She had come damn close to fooling Wes!

CHAPTER XIII

He studied the heavy oak door. There was a half inch crack at the bottom where late afternoon sun fanned across the stone floor. He gave silent thanks that the place was a powder magazine and not a real jail with a judas hole in the door. Nor was there a keyhole since it was padlocked with a hasp on the outside. Until he saw the shadow of a foot under that door, until he heard a key in the lock, Wes was absolutely alone. He straightened out the brown wrapping paper he'd used to wipe his hands and face, then began using the bottle of lemon juice and toothpicks.

Within moments he had done all that can be asked of mortal man and organic chemistry. He wrapped the empty plate in the dirty paper, making a separate package of the wheat-sheaved fork and spoon. He left the handles sticking out to save Ford the trouble of unwrapping to make sure his prisoner was not high-grading a potential weapon. He put everything back in the basket and put the basket by the door. Then he went back to lie supine on the straw tick and gaze at the distant roof.

It was such a faint chance, it was hardly a chance at all. He wondered if he was grasping at straws, seeing patterns and reasons where there were none. Had he done everything possible? If he were to stand someday in the morning sun with a rope around his neck and suddenly to remember something else he might have done, Wes knew he was going to feel pretty put out about it.

He lay back and tried to sleep. Some hours later, to his faint surprise, he discovered that he had. It was night, with a darkness as total as he had experienced in the mine. The straw tick's natives were out in full force. Scratching, he realized they were what had roused him. He sat up in the darkness, swinging his bad leg with more than usual awkwardness.

Had Ford removed the empty basket? He felt blindly, crawling until he touched a wall and made a circuit of the room, crisscrossing until he was sure he had covered every square inch. The basket was gone. Everything now depended on whether Ford would prefer not to dirty his fingers with used utensils. Depended also, Wes soberly realized, on whether he was letting his imagination run away. He might be as wrong about this as he seemed to have been about every other important decision in his life.

This decision, if he had guessed right, was going to let him in for an inevitable series of obligations and responsibilities. He tried not to think too deeply of where it would all end. In a way, it was more comforting to dwell upon the noose that waited if he had guessed wrong. He scratched and offered a silent opinion of the All-powerful Intelligence that had seen fit to create the myriad inhabitants of this straw tick.

> He prayeth well, who loveth well
> Both man and bird and beast.

> He prayeth best, who loveth best
> All things both great and small;
> For the dear God who loveth us,
> He made and loveth all.

Were Coleridge and his creation to debate the subject,

Wes suspected the Ancient Mariner's opinion of bedbugs would lie closer to his own than to the poet's. He scratched in the dark and wondered if he would sleep better on the stone floor. Probably not. They were all over him now so he might as well enjoy the straw tick. He was just stretching out again when he heard the sound of metal sliding past unoiled metal. A moment later the padlock opened and door hinges creaked.

"Mr. Brooks?"

"Who?" Wes whispered.

"Tinacling."

So the Indian boy had remembered the name Wes gave him. Hastily, he stuffed feet into boots and moved toward the slightly brighter rectangle of the open door. "Who sent you?" Wes whispered into the boy's ear.

"I did, Mr. Brooks." It was Miss Upton's voice.

Wes wondered if he had done the right thing. "Sorry I had to drag you into it," he murmured.

"I'm afraid you had little choice," the girl said. "There's a watch on my house. We'd better leave before they discover I'm gone."

But Tinacling was lugging something heavy into the cell. They waited in the darkness until he came out again and closed the padlock. Wes wondered momentarily, then realized that, like railroad padlocks, the mining company locks probably all opened with the same key. After all, it had been a powder magazine and not a jail.

"Thanks for believing me," he murmured as the silent trio oozed down the single street of Opal. "I wasn't sure that lemon juice would work."

"Perfectly legible with ten minutes in the oven," the girl said. "But I nearly scorched the paper trying to read your greasy thumb prints."

"I'm sorry about your father."

"So am I," the girl said with an air of finality.

Despite the mine's unceasing three shifts, there was nobody else on the street this time of night. They moved away from the headframe, heading downhill toward the office-residence where first Wes had broken bread with Miss Upton and her father. "But aren't they watching there?" he asked.

He could barely see his companions despite having his eyes used to darkness apart from the tiny flicker of spark for an instant before Tinacling had locked the jail door. He didn't see the narrow opening between a pair of darkened buildings until the girl grasped his elbow and guided him in. They stood silent and tense in the darkness and Wes was abruptly aware of the smell of red hair at close range. It was a very agreeable smell.

Uphill bells jangled and the hoisting engine chuffed another load of unrefined riches to the surface. Wes tried to remember the list of things he had written with toothpick and lemon juice on the brown paper that had enclosed his lunch. As the trio stood in the dark waiting for God only knew what, he wondered how many articles on the list the girl and the Indian boy had been able to accumulate. It couldn't have been easy under the suspicious eyes of Ford and Green Eyeshade.

Suddenly there was the popping of pistols. Then he knew there couldn't be that many pistols in the whole county. It was a string of firecrackers. Before he could wonder if this infantile diversion was going to fool anybody the sound of firecrackers was drowned out in the dull, roaring boom of a heavier explosion. The roof came off the powder magazine-jail he had just left. He wondered if the explosion had taken off only the roof or if it would have burst the heavy door too. But mostly he wondered if the people thronging the single street would all stampede uphill to see what had happened—or would some laggard stop to look into the darkness between two houses where the three of them cowered?

After the cave-in the residents of Opal were gun-shy, turning out at the slightest disturbance whether or not the whistle summoned them. The town was dark, catching only the faintest glimmer of the carbide lights up around the headframe. The light was enough for him to see the citizenry streaming uphill. Still they hung back, crouching in the darkness.

Then he saw the unmistakable profile of a puffy-faced man in too-small derby puffing uphill and, three paces behind him, the green-eyeshaded station agent. They waited a minute longer. "Now," the boy in black braids breathed.

They stepped out and for the first time Wes noted that Miss Upton was wearing men's clothing, with her abundant hair stuffed up inside a slightly oversized Stetson. Casually, they strolled downhill, past the Opal Mining and Development Company's office, down to the false-fronted arch that guarded the stage company's corral.

Somebody—Tinacling, Wes supposed, had saddled the lead team and the off-wheeler. While the boy and Miss Upton mounted without fuss Wes studied the stirrup and tried to decide which was the easiest way for a stiff-legged man to mount. Finally, with a prayer that the wheeler would stand for such shenanigans, he twisted the stirrup, got his foot into it, and swung aboard with his bad leg windmilling grotesquely over the horse's back. The horse apparently didn't care.

They urged the horses out through the archway and down the single street. He glanced back and saw that Tinacling was leading the extra member of the stage's four-horse team. "Any other horses in town?" Wes asked.

"I hope not," Miss Upton said. "Do you ride any better than you drive?"

"Don't know," Wes said. "I haven't tried it in nineteen years." He was about to say something else when there was a shout and a shot behind them. A bullet ricocheted and went skittering down Opal's single street past them, and then he was too busy trying to stay with a galloping horse for any further conversation.

With each jolt something was banging against his knee. The galloping horses reached the lower end of Opal where houses faced the single street at odd angles and he saw the woman who had waved and beckoned standing in her doorway, a half-clad man beside her as they stared uphill toward the headframe and the noise.

Now that he had gotten out of the jail-magazine, Wes wondered where next. He hadn't counted on the Indian boy coming along. He wondered if Tinacling had burnt his bridges behind him. Probably. If he hadn't before, surely somebody would have noticed those black braids flying in the dawn air as four horses galloped for the lives of three humans.

They had galloped well past the last house now, following the stage road toward the county seat when finally the horses slowed to a walk. "Anybody know where we're going?" Wes asked. Tinacling and Miss Upton drew up abruptly and looked at him.

"Don't you, Mr. Brooks?" the girl asked.

It struck Wes abruptly that this capable young lady was taking a lot on faith. "I just had to get you out of there before you had a slip of the tongue and—" He left it dangling.

There was a moment of silence, then, "Exactly what happened, Mr. Brooks?" the girl asked.

Wes told her.

"So they're both in it," she mused, "Ford and Polk."

It was Wes's first inkling that the green-eyeshaded stage agent was related to the shrill man down in the county seat who had hired him. He did not find the news encouraging.

"You know the sheriff?" he asked. "A man named Hurley?"

Miss Upton did not. "I've been gone for some years," she reminded.

"I do," Tinacling said.

"Is he an honest man?"

The Indian boy gave Wes an odd look. "Me no speak English too good," he said. "What that word mean?"

Wes sighed. "Miss Upton and I are both white," he finally said.

"Inside?" Tinacling asked.

They rode in silence, squinting into the rising sun. Wes turned to the girl. "'Scuse my askin'," he said tentatively. "But if I was you, I wonder if I'd believe me."

The girl concentrated on urging her horse along at a fast trot. The boy rode gracefully as he did everything else, studying the two of them and offering no comment.

"There is the question of motive, I suppose," Miss Upton finally said. "I don't really believe you've been involved in our affairs long enough to get into a gold-stealing conspiracy. On the surface it would seem senseless for a man to side against his benefactors."

"You suspected Ford and, uh—Polk?"

"There is the principle of *cui bono*."

"Didn't know you was a lawyer too."

"I'm not," the girl said shortly. "But Father's money gave me a force-feeding of Latin. What it means is, Who stands to gain?"

"Just about anybody, I'd guess," Wes hazarded.

"Not exactly." The girl looked behind. It was still half dark behind them and difficult to see if they were being followed. They urged the horses on, on past the place where he had found old Gabe bloody and lifeless. Wes could feel himself starting to chafe in places where a sergeant of infantry normally does not. And he sensed that some of the straw tick's inhabitatnts had joined him in his journey.

"Gold coins are one thing," the girl added. "Bullion is something else. A half century ago gold dust was negotiable in this country. Every store and saloon had gold scales. But even then few people carried bullion."

Wes saw what she was getting at. To get rid of a gold brick might turn out to be even harder than stealing it. "Banks," he mused. "And maybe the Treasury?"

"Exactly," Miss Upton said. "With paperwork and lengthy pedigrees."

"So that's why you decided I didn't kill your father?" Wes asked.

"Only partly," the Indian boy said unexpectedly. "You see, I was peeking through the keyhole when Ford shot him."

CHAPTER XIV

Wes pondered this for a moment, feeling slightly deflated at the knowledge that it hadn't been his sterling character that had convinced the girl of his innocence. Then he saw the silver lining. "We're home free," he said. "We've got a witness."

"I'm afraid not," the girl said.

Wes dug his spurless heels into the wheeler in an effort to keep up. "The judge and sheriff crooked too?" he asked.

"I don't know," Miss Upton said. "After all, I'm nearly as much of a stranger here as you."

While Wes digested this the boy clarified their legal position. "You're talkin' just like I was a white man," he said. "But I'm not. If you're going to get along in this country, Mr. Brooks, you may's well learn a ward of the government can't testify any more'n a dog or a horse can."

"And we're living in modern times," Wes muttered. "Nineteen-oh-two!"

Tinacling's broad, flat face was looking behind them. Wes concentrated on urging his wheeler to keep up, then finally realized that a wheel horse could only feel right trotting behind the others, that no amount of encouragement was going to make the poor beast feel natural trotting abreast. He looked over his shoulder and the country behind them was growing lighter now until he guessed he would be able to see anyone chasing. He could not. He wondered where they were going to go. "You know any safe place?" he asked the boy in black braids.

Tinacling gave him an odd look. "Plenty of room up in the hills if you want to hide up there and watch somebody else eat and drink while we starve."

Wes looked at the girl. She looked back. "No easy way, Mr. Brooks," she said. "I fear you are my only champion."

From this capable young lady it was a startling admission. While Wes stared, she added, "You see, in a way I too am a ward of the government. Though my testimony may be admissible under certain circumstances, I cannot vote. Also, it's possible that a court may judge me incompetent and appoint someone else to administer my estate."

Wes whistled. "Isn't there any way you can get around that?" he asked.

"Only one," Miss Upton said in a strange, flat voice.

They rode along in silence and Tinacling kept glancing back. Wes wished he understood a little more about civil law. But in the army he had lived by another set of rules. "Excuse me for askin'," he said, "but how old are you, Miss Upton?"

"Oh that's not the problem," the girl said. "I've attained my majority by any standard. In fact, at twenty-five I'm perilously close to having missed the boat."

No more so than Wes was, he mused. His body was unused to riding and the myriad bug bites did little to increase his comfort, yet for a moment he dwelt on the china-blue-eyed, red-haired memory of a warrant officer's daughter who had grown up wise in the ways of the army. He remembered how calmly she had sat beside a hospital bed and told him she would never marry a sergeant—not even one with two good legs and a future. Whatever had happened to her? With any luck she would have made her catch by now. With a vague sense of wonder Wes discov-

ered that he wasn't even bitter any more. He wished her
well, hoped the warrant officer's daughter had managed to
forget him sooner than he had her.

"Mr. Brooks!"

"Uh—sorry. Did you say something?"

"You didn't answer my question, Mr. Brooks."

"Guess I didn't. My mind was on something else. What
was it you asked?" Wes asked.

"A very simple question," Miss Upton said. "Will you
marry me?"

"Oh, my God!" Wes replied.

"*He* can't vote either," Miss Upton said. "That's why I'm
asking you."

Wes felt his face and shoulders turn a dull red. He remembered the rage he had swallowed whenever some officer
had issued a more than usually stupid order, when a young
lieutenant had preferred to throw away the unhallowed lives
of enlisted men rather than accept the most tactfully worded
suggestion. For nineteen years he had put up with it in the
army.

The Indian boy would put up with it as long as he lived,
his destiny and his very life in the hands of strangers less
competent than himself. And this was what it was like to be
a woman, Wes realized. Miss Upton, intelligent, educated,
born to property and position. And she was humiliated—
reduced to begging a penniless stranger to marry her.

"I'm sorry," he said.

"You won't marry me?"

"Of course I will if it'll help. I'm just sorry you had to do
it this way." He paused and added, "But is there any
preacher around here—any way to make it legal?"

Wes and Miss Upton both looked to Tinacling for an answer, but the boy was still looking behind them. Wes turned

and saw what he was looking at. "Thought there weren't any more horses in Opal," he groused.

Nobody answered him. They were all too busy studying the boiling dust cloud behind them. There was enough dust for half a regiment of cavalry. Where, Wes wondered, had they all come from? He thought a moment and decided there couldn't be that many people in on the high-grading scam. If there were it would never have remained a secret this long. Then, in answer to his unspoken question Miss Upton said, "They'll have said you kidnapped me, Mr. Brooks. Perhaps if I were to lag behind you could get away."

"And you could die from an accidental bullet before you had a chance to tell all those well-meaning citizens what's really going on," Wes snapped. He yelled and kicked his spurless heels into the wheeler's flanks.

"Where'd they get the horses?" Tinacling asked.

"From underground probably," the girl said. "And if we can just stay ahead of them until the sun's brighter . . ."

Blind horses, Wes realized, so many years underground they would be helpless in the light of day. He had felt handicapped on stagecoach harness horses. But their pursuing posse was mounted on even worse stock that had spent years hauling ore underground in the bigger drifts where there was room for a horse. He yelled again and kicked his heels. The wheeler held its position behind the girl and the Indian boy on the lead horses.

It was hopeless. The stage horses were in better shape and could outrun the others but—to where? Even if there were some place to hide, they could not get enough head start to lose the blundering, thundering mob behind them. Tinacling and Miss Upton managed to urge their horses into an easy gallop and Wes's wheeler obligingly broke into a gallop to keep pace.

They broke out onto the flat where he had dug his well and set up his tent. Here, there was even less cover. His tent hung motionless in the still, morning air, its shreds reminiscent of some lost battle of frontier days. And he had been going to make a new life for himself in this country!

He looked behind and the dust cloud was much smaller now. Winded, he guessed. The horses from underground had been pulling ore cars for as long as their equine memories could function. On the surface, dazzled blind, galloping for the first time in their lives, most of them had come to a sweaty rib-heaving halt. But half a dozen of the hardiest still pursued a couple of miles behind Wes and his companions.

Beside him the unmounted wheeler galloped, holding position as if the four horses were still harnessed. The girl glanced over her shoulder. "I believe," she remarked, "that in situations like this, one tosses the baby to the wolves."

Tinacling's face as he glanced at Miss Upton suggested he was only now discovering she was really white. Wes was still wondering exactly what the girl had in mind when abruptly she produced a small-caliber pistol and fired several rapid shots into the air, simultaneously reining up.

The other three horses tried to stop too. "No," the girl urged. "Keep moving. Can't you see I'm making my escape?"

Wes and the Indian boy looked at each other. "I can't let you do it," Wes said. "They might kill you."

"Not if you put enough distance between us," the girl said. "There're too many people watching. Hurry up now or it'll be too late."

The half-dozen diehard pursuers were drawing closer while Wes and the girl wrangled. He shrugged. Everything else had gone wrong. Why shouldn't this? He yelled and dug his spurless heels into the wheeler. Tinacling slapped reins over his horse's rump and they were once more galloping, doing their best to use the time the girl had bought them by turning back.

"Some days you just can't make a dime," Wes growled.
"An hour ago you were waitin' to be hung," Tinacling said, his broad face low over the neck of the lead horse.

Wes yelled and slapped reins until finally he had forced his wheeler abreast. He was hurting in every joint, his abraded, bug-chewed skin promising even greater torments if ever this ride were to end. He supposed the boy was right. The only difference was, now he and the boy would both be hung. And the girl? He wondered how wide a trail she had left behind, getting him out of the powder magazine? Would anybody believe she had been kidnapped, that she had just this minute managed her escape?

There were two men in Opal who would not believe a word of it. But would Ford and Polk dare do anything in plain sight? Perhaps not. If the company bull and the stage agent were to doubt Miss Upton's story too openly somebody up in Opal might decide to ask what really happened.

He risked a backward glance and saw the pursuit had stopped as the girl reached the men behind them. And in the instant he had stopped urging his horse the wheeler had dropped back into its usual position following the horse the boy was riding. "What we gonna do now?" the boy asked over his shoulder.

How the hell am I supposed to know? Wes almost voiced his sentiments, but he had been a sergeant too long. "Keep moving," he grunted. At least he was free; the boy was free. Was he any better off than before, when he had been locked up and the boy had still been able to move freely about Opal, listening and peeping?

Wes guessed so. There wasn't too much more to be

learned in Opal. There was only one other town of any consequence in this country and they were heading for it. Polk . . . there were two of them—in charge of each end of the stage line. Should've known something was wrong when that shrill little man in Okapogum had suddenly turned fawning and offered him an unbelievable hundred dollars a month.

Was everybody in this damned county crooked? What about Hurley? Was there any safe way to sound out the sheriff? He remembered that red-mustached man's readiness with a gun. And the only weapon Wes now possessed was the Sharps that was wearing his leg rawer with each step of this trotting wheeler.

Once the news reached Okapogum, there would be no converse between Wes and the sheriff, save over the sights of their weapons. If he were to talk things over and try to smell out where the sheriff's sympathies lay, it would have to be soon—before the mob got to the county seat with the news.

For one sinking moment of total depression Wes wondered if there might be a telephone or heliograph to trip him up. Then he remembered that Ford and Polk had sent the news about the last holdup by stage, by Wes. If he could manage not to fall off this horse for another fifteen miles, maybe he could have a quiet conversation with Hurley.

He studied the boy on the lead horse in front of him. Tinacling rode as effortlessly as he walked. Anywhere else in the world, in any other skin the boy would be a trick rider or trapeze artist, perhaps even some sort of a dancer. Here, if he were to stick with Wes he would end up either in jail or dead. "Isn't there some place you can go?" Wes asked. "It isn't your fight."

Tinacling turned. "Where do you expect me to go?" he asked. "I know they say an Indian always goes back to the blanket, but can you guess how far from the blanket I've come to speak this kind of English?"

Wes could guess. He, too, had come a long way from the security of his army blanket. "Welcome to the universal brotherhood of man," he grunted.

"Yeah," Tinacling said. "And you'd better get set to meet a few more brothers." The Indian boy was looking straight ahead.

CHAPTER XV

Wes stared over the wheeler's bobbing head. Ahead of them, nearly at the edge of the flat were four mounted men. "Impossible," he muttered. The Opal mob on blind horses couldn't possibly have gotten around them. He looked behind. There was nobody there. He didn't know whether they had given up and turned back to Opal with their prize or if he had already ridden out of sight of where the girl had delayed pursuit.

"Who d'you suppose it is?" he asked.

Tinacling didn't know. "If it was stage day I'd say you were going to get robbed again."

Without instruction and constant reminders the horses had slowed to a fast walk. Wes didn't know the quality of horseflesh up ahead, but he knew the stagecoach horses were tired and not riding stock to begin with. There was no turning back toward Opal. It would be equally pointless to strike out in any other direction to avoid four men waiting on fresh horses.

Now that the wheeler was walking, Wes's total consciousness was not devoted just to hanging on. He remembered the last time he had waited for somebody else to shoot first. Someday, perhaps, Okapogum County would be sufficiently civilized for strangers not to shoot on sight. But not, apparently, in nineteen-oh-two.

He got the Sharps out of the boot, which had been made for a much shorter rifle. The four strangers were still five

hundred yards away, waiting impassively for Wes and Tinacling to come closer. Wes checked the rifle while the horse
ambled another hundred yards. Then he reined his wheeler
to a halt. The horse stood placid as a politician in office
while Wes shouldered the Sharps. He took his time aiming.
Even when he fired sideways from the saddle the wheeler
hardly flinched.

Up ahead there was sudden commotion among the four
horses, followed by a staccato popping of hand guns. Tinacling swung down on the safe side of his leader until he was
exposing only the sole of one bare foot and a fist gripping a
saddle horn. Wes applied Kentucky windage and put another round into the quartet ahead of him. And suddenly
they were galloping off at right angles to the road, one man
drooping ungracefully as another caught the reins of his
horse.

"How'd you know they'd run away?" Tinacling asked.

"Didn't," Wes said. "Only figured they were at least as
smart as I am."

The boy looked a question.

"Range," Wes explained. "Even if they didn't know a
Sharps when they heard one, they had to know it was a
rifle." He shrugged and added, "Wasn't any need to duck
like you did. There's no pistol made could hit anything until
they got twice as close."

"And you knew it," Tinacling marveled.

"So did they," Wes said. "Now let's just pray they don't
turn out to be nice lawabidin' citizens who'll get down to
town before we do and go spreadin' all kinds of tales about
how unfriendly we are."

"Oh Jesus!" the boy muttered. Wes was inclined to agree.
He felt around the too-short scabbard and found cartridges.
When the rifle was reloaded and jammed back into the
boot, he urged the patient wheeler back into motion.

"Wonder how Miss Alberdeen's making out," Tinacling wondered as they approached the drop-off at the edge of the flat.

Wes had been thinking his own dark thoughts, and it took him a moment to realize that Miss Alberdeen was also Miss Upton. She had managed to reach their pursuers without any shooting. But how long could she stay alive in a town where Ford and Polk controlled everything—where they had murdered her father without hesitation?

They approached the drop-off with its series of switchbacks that were not quite so hair raising as the final drop down to the level of the river. And Wes was still wrapped in his own thoughts when the Indian boy muttered, "More damn people in this country lately." Wes looked up and the boy was pointing downhill.

Halfway down the drop-off a man was walking. Limping. He seemed on the edge of exhaustion. The horses started down the road, blowing and scattering pebbles with their broad hooves and the man ahead was so sunk in dejection that he didn't even look up. Wes wondered if this stranger had seen the bandits or if that quartet had assembled after he had passed. Then it occurred to him that the men he had scattered with the Sharps might be responsible for this man's pedestrian condition. "Somebody steal your horse?" Wes asked as they caught up with the stumbling stranger.

The man looked up with vague, unfocused eyes and saw Wes. "You!" he exploded.

"Me? I got enough troubles without stealin' somebody else's horses." As he said it, Wes abruptly realized he was guilty of that, too. The man who glared up at him seemed vaguely familiar. "Swear I'd seen you before somewhere," Wes added.

Saying it, he realized where he had seen this bedraggled stranger before. He had seen him by the light of carbide lamps, perched on a pile of stulls trying to talk the muckers of the Opal mine into striking. This was the man whose performance Wes had ruined, who had departed Opal amid a shower of offal.

They stared at each other, each struggling to decide what to say next. "You got about ten more miles to town," Wes finally said. "And we got an extra horse. Only fair to warn you people're liable to start shootin' at us."

"So what else is new?" the agitator grumbled as he climbed stiffly aboard the other wheeler. He was still smeared with various semiliquescent substances thrown at him by the citizens of Opal.

They rode in silence for the better part of a mile, down the drop-off and onto the next flat. "Who's shootin' at you?" the stranger finally asked.

"Kind of a long and complicated story," Wes said. "Did you meet any strangers on the road?"

The filth-encrusted man had not.

"Whatever got into you to start trouble at a mine ready to close down anyhow?" Wes prodded. "It's one thing to be crazy, but I never thought the union was stupid."

"Close down!" the organizer exploded. "More gold's come out of that mine in the last year than in any other five! If Upton's closing down, then you're callin' the wrong man stupid."

"Could be," Wes said equably. "But he's also dead."

"No!" The organizer's surprise was deflatingly total. He stared at Wes a moment, then his eyes narrowed. "He was alive when I left town. You ain't layin' it on me."

"No chance," Wes agreed. "They're layin' it on somebody else."

"Anybody I know?"

Wes shrugged. "He just lent you a horse."

The stranger regarded Wes as if he had just sprouted fangs. "You?"

"I didn't say I did it," Wes amended. "No more than you ever said you worked underground."

"Whose side are you on?"

"Number one," Wes said.

The filth-besmeared man regarded Wes pityingly. "Isn't much to live or die for, is it?"

"It's all I got."

There was a long silence and finally the stranger began in a monotone. "You're right about me never working underground. Never worked anywhere!" he added savagely. "Do you claim a monopoly on the dark night of the soul?"

Wes studied the man in silence.

"Comes the day people grow up, pull their heads out of the sand and see that every idol has feet of clay."

"You sound like you just lost an election."

"I've lost many things—so many that all I have left is a belief in people. Imperfect, less-than-gods, but better than their creations."

"Creations?" Wes echoed. "You don't sound like a soldier."

"Their churches and their gods," the other man thundered, his eyes ablaze with an abrupt Jehovic wrath. "Before I became an organizer, before I learned some basic facts about this world we live in, I was a man of God. Tell me sir, have you never yearned to bring the word of Wealth to the poor benighted heathen?"

"No," Wes admitted. "My specialty was spreading civilization with a Krag."

"Welcome to the brotherhood of the damned," Tinacling said unexpectedly. "And which of you worthy gentlemen's presence besmirches the other?"

"My God," Wes grunted, "are you a preacher, too?"

"Would have been if I'd been able to stick it out," the boy admitted. "Where do you think I learned all this lovely English?"

Wes was suddenly nervous riding between two men of God. He managed to refrain from saying the obvious. The trio rode across the last flat before the terrifying descent to the river and county seat. Ahead in the shimmering distance he saw the dusty cottonwoods that lined the creek. He squinted and wondered if it was hotter there. Then he realized the shimmer was from a nearly invisible column of smoke that climbed unwaveringly skyward.

"Can't swing a cat anymore without hittin' somebody in this country," Tinacling grumbled. "I can remember when there wasn't a soul within miles."

"How long ago was that?" Wes asked.

"About six months," the boy said.

Wes studied the reeking man on the other wheeler. Cleaned up, perhaps he could be of some use. Might send him into town ahead with a note for Hurley . . . get the red-mustached sheriff out somewhere in neutral territory where they could sound one another out. But he didn't like the glint in that too-wide eye.

Wes rode toward the creek and the rising smoke, paying little attention to his surroundings. In this open country, there was slight chance of ambush. If he could find out where the sheriff stood. If Hurley was as capable of hiding behind a corkscrew as every other crook in this county, Wes didn't know what he was going to do.

"At it again," Tinacling muttered.

Wes glanced up, but the boy didn't elaborate so he returned to his circular reasoning. Ford and Polk—the Polks, he amended, had been working some kind of a fiddle at the mine or possibly inside the smelter. Somehow gold had been shortstopped before it reached Upton. The company bull and his crew had been skimming so much the mine was in danger of going broke—and laying all the blame on the stage robbers.

And the bandits thought Wes was doing it. Even if he were to square himself with Hurley and the law, Wes knew he would never know a moment's peace in this country until he either captured the bandits or convinced them that it was somebody else who had been robbing honest bandits of the fruit of their labor.

Beside him the organizer began singing "Solidarity Forever" in an unmelodious voice. "There'll be water up ahead," Wes hinted. "Why don't you save your voice till then?"

There was a moment of silence and then the former preacher was declaiming.

"Doth then the world go thus, doth all thus move?
Is this the justice which on Earth we find?
Is this that firm decree which all doth bind?
Are these your influences, Powers above?
Those souls which vice's moody mists most blind,
Blind Fortune, blindly, most their friend doth prove,
And they who thee, poor idol Virtue! love,
Ply like a feather toss'd by storm and wind.
Ah! if a Providence doth sway this all
Why should best minds groan under most distress?
Or why should pride humility make thrall,
And injuries the innocent oppress?
Heavens! hinder, stop this fate; or grant a time
When good may have, as well as bad, their prime!"

There was an appropriate pause and then the preacher cackled, "Bet you don't know who wrote that."

"Would you like to bet it was William Drummond's sonnets that called me right out of the seminary?" Tinacling asked.

Wes was startled out of his reverie. Of all the times and places to discuss God's ways with man . . . He looked around the flat. The sage grew thicker as they approached the cottonwoods, but there was still not enough cover for an ambush. He studied the rising column of heat and nearly invisible smoke that rose from amid the cottonwoods, wondering what required so steady a flame. Some squatter boiling soap?

"Bet you don't know," the filth-encrusted preacher cackled, turning to Wes.

For an instant Wes thought he was asking about the smoke, then he remembered the sonnet. Could this renegade preacher ever imagine the scarcity of books, the utter boredom that assailed a thinking man in any army outpost? "Drummond was a Scotsman, friend of Ben Jonson," he said. "His sonnets were published the year Shakespeare died." As he said it Wes realized this was not all he knew on the subject. Studying the filthy man beside him, he knew without a doubt that the ex-preacher was nutty as a fruitcake.

CHAPTER XVI

So there went his idea of sending this man into town to contact Hurley. The unfortunate preacher had lost his faith in God, and after his reception in Opal there couldn't remain much faith in any brotherhood of man. A day or two walking across these dry flats with neither food nor water couldn't have contributed much toward his stability. "There's water and shade up ahead," Wes said reassuringly. But privately, he suspected any opportunity to lead this man beside the still waters had come several years too late. If he didn't keep a tight rein on his imagination, Wes suspected he too might eventually conclude that a whole world conspired against him, that every pebble and burr was created for his unique annoyance. He had seen it happen to better men.

What was he going to do? In spite of his best efforts to remain aloof from this country and these people's problems, everything conspired to draw him in deeper. He remembered Miss Upton's proposal of marriage. Or had it been a proposition?

He hadn't been around women that much. Flighty as horses they were—most of them anyway. Still, a flighty woman was only an annoyance. But her calm evaluation of life as it is and not as it ought to be . . . Miss Alberdeen Upton was not annoying; she was frightening. What story was she telling the denizens of Opal now? One thing for damned sure—she was not telling them she had asked her kidnapper to marry her.

At least he would get into Okapogum first, before somebody else had a chance to bend Hurley's ear. Then Wes had his first flash of inspiration. In the army it was axiomatic that the first liar didn't have a chance. He knew Ford and the Polks were in on it. Who else? They were not the sort to risk their own necks when somebody else's could be used— like Wes's. As the trio approached the ford where the ancient and bewhiskered Mr. Bridges had twice stopped the stage, Wes abruptly decided he would not go down that final hair-raising stretch of road into Okapogum. It would be far more instructive to camp here in the shade of the cottonwoods and see who was first down the road from Opal with the news.

This time the resident troll was not on hand to receive them. While men and horses drank at the creek Wes studied the impenetrable cottonwood thickets. Somewhere upstream that column of smoke was still rising, though he could not see it from here. They finished drinking except for the preacher who wallowed fully clothed in the cool water, scrubbing ineffectually at the dried filth that surrounded him. Wes walked back out onto the road and studied the flat behind them. Nobody coming. The smoke was a good quarter mile upstream.

He glanced back down into the ford and saw that Tinacling had already taken charge of the horses, leading them upstream out of sight and picketing the beasts where they could graze and drink again. Wes began working his way upstream along the more penetrable outer fringe of cottonwoods. He guessed he was within a hundred yards of the smoke when he heard the voice from somewhere behind him. "Where's your stage, young feller?"

Caught again. It reminded Wes that he was by no means

the young feller that he had once been. Turning carefully, he saw it was the buckskinned and bewhiskered Mr. Bridges. Perhaps from that ancient's viewpoint he was still a "young feller." In any event, the old man had his venerable Hawken again, the muzzle pointing fairly closely toward Wes.

"Your place?" Wes asked. "Boilin' soap?" But even as he asked the questions Wes finally knew what the fire was. Even if he hadn't been able by now to smell the by-products of fermentation, there were few cottage industries left these days that required a smokeless fire, could be conducted with noiseless, no-moving-parts machinery, but were always located near running water to cool the worm. "Should have guessed sooner," Wes muttered. "Can't they see it or smell it down in town?"

"Live and let live," Bridges cackled, lowering the rifle. "Where's the stage?"

"Didn't bring it this trip," Wes said, then realized he was facing a possible source of information. "You looked inside the stage that first day and come out lookin' like a cat with a mouthful of canary feathers. Said I'd get a royal welcome down in Okapogum. The funny thing is, that's just what I got."

The oldster squinted at Wes. "Everything goin' just fine now, ain't it?"

Wes wondered if the old man knew about his shoot-outs with bandits. There was no way he could know what had happened up in Opal. "You seemed friendly with Miss Upton," he probed. "Were you a friend of her paw's?"

"Why don't you ask him?"

Wes sighed. He could play games forever with this old coot who was at least half as mad as the renegade preacher. "I would," he confessed, "except Mr. Upton died before I got a chance."

"Well now, I'm downright sorry to hear that. Feelin' poorly, was he?"

"He didn't die a natural death. Does anybody ever in this country?"

"You're learnin'," the old man said. "Who done him in?"

Wes knew now he should have brought the Sharps with him. But if he had, the old man would have been convinced of unfriendly intentions and Wes would already be dead. "You're gonna hear it soon anyway," he said. "You might as well get it from me first."

"You killed Upton?"

"Ford did it while I and Polk watched. The two of them're layin' it onto me."

"Serves you right."

"I s'pose so. If I'd figured it out a second sooner, Upton might still be alive. What kind of a man is Hurley?"

"He's the sheriff."

"I know that," Wes said tiredly.

"See'd 'em once," the old man reminisced. "Gold in the strongbox. Gold everywhere. Even gold under the seat cushions. See'd 'em with my own two eyes a liftin' them bricks out. I figured 'twarn't none o' my business. Andrew Upton don't know his own people are swindlin' him, he got no business runnin' a mine."

For an instant Wes thought he meant the sheriff, but the old man was talking about bandits. "You know their names?"

"Sure do," Bridges cackled. "Know how many you shot too."

Wes wondered if the old man knew about the one he had captured in his room—the one Ford had shot while "escaping."

Imperceptibly in the course of this conversation they had moved deeper into the cottonwoods until they came within sight of the still. The old man put his ear as close to the thump keg as he could without burning it and listened intently. He fed a couple of sticks of well-dried cottonwood to the fire and the drip down the wooden sliver in the cold end of the worm became faster. "Drink?" he offered.

Wes surveyed the warm, minutes-old liquid and shook his head. He'd been here for several minutes now. He was going to have to set watch-on-watch with Tinacling if they were to intercept whoever came bearing the news from Opal. He glanced around and the Indian boy was already studying the still with an expressionless face. At that moment the stranger, sopping wet and his clothes still spotted with filth, burst into the tiny clearing. He took in the installation with a single glance. "Demon rum!" the stranger said in his cracked voice. "The Curse of the Working Class!"

" 'Tain't rum," the old man cackled. "It's whiskey."

But the labor organizer had seen enough. He turned and went splashing back down the creek. Wes shrugged and went out of the thicket where he could study the road from Opal. Still no sign of anybody. The boy appeared beside him. "Old man been at this very long?" Wes asked.

"Long as I can remember," Tinacling said. "At least he's honest."

Wes looked at him.

"Value for money," the boy said. "You know it's against the law for an Indian to drink good whiskey, don't you?"

Wes guessed he had known. "Against the law to sell any kind to an Indian, isn't it?"

"That may have been the purpose of the law," Tinacling said bitterly. "But in practice it means white men get the good stuff and we pay three times as much for poison. About the best you can say about Bridges' hooch is nobody ever went blind from it. Old man's kind of particular about selling to drunks and known troublemakers too."

Wes could see where the grizzled ancient served a purpose in the community. His reverie was interrupted by the
sound of the demented preacher's voice loudly proclaiming
that the mark of the beast is 666 and other debatable premises from Revelations.

The boy looked expressionlessly at Wes. "Damned if I
know what to do with him," Wes admitted. "Any civilized
country they'd lock him up but out here . . ." Out here,
Wes suspected, the addled organizer wasn't really that much
farther out than the average citizen at the end of the winter
and cabin-fever season.

"Hungry?" It was Bridges who had followed them to the
edge of the thicket. "Knocked over a buck a couple of days
ago. On'y thing is, I got to tend the still till this run's over."
The ancient paused and added, "Startin' to feel a mite
peaked myself."

Wes looked at the boy. "I'll stand first watch," Tinacling
offered. Wes nodded and followed Bridges back to the still.
"Cabin's thataway," Bridges said, listening once more at the
thump keg.

Wes nodded and followed the path. He could smell the
cabin before he saw it. Somewhere down by the ford, the
preacher was still calling down hellfire and brimstone. Wes
tried to breathe shallow as he opened the door of the
lowroofed cabin. He had seen and smelled the disorganized
squalor of dirty old men before. The horror that lay always
in the back of his mind was that, if he were to live long
enough, Wes too might end up living in some similar rat's
nest of filth and stench—of chores postponed until an old
man had more time, until he felt better, until the weather
improved.

He got a fire going in the stone hearth that took up one
whole end of the jumble of sodden blankets, greasy skillets-
ful of rat turds, the sweetish stench of manhood gone to

seed. After a moment the fire began drawing fresh air through the open door and he could breathe easier.

Wes gathered up an armful of utensils and went down to the creek to scrub them with sand. Ought to give that still-ranting preacher something to do, he guessed. But he had enough on his mind without coping with a man who had apparently lost his last vestige of sanity walking across the sere flats from Opal.

"For if any man see thee which hast knowledge sit at meat in the idol's temple, shall not the conscience of him which is weak be emboldened to eat those things which are offered to idols?"

Hearing that cracked voice cry in the wilderness, Wes guessed he might as well not bother asking the preacher for help. He scrubbed the insides of pots and skillets clean, knowing it would take hours or perhaps days to remove the years' accumulation of grease-compacted soot from their outer surfaces.

There was a limbed-off cottonwood near the cabin door. He undid the rope and lowered the deer carcass below the fly line long enough to hack off a meal, then hoisted it again. After a spell outside, the dirty-old-man stench of the cabin was overpowering again. The meat was not as young as it might have been either. He sniffed at the stringy collops and decided upon a stew instead of frying.

The fire had settled down nicely by now. When the venison was simmering, he poked about and to his delight discovered that Mr. Bridges actually had some still-edible onions. He was sitting in the doorway peeling them when he realized the meat would have to cook for some time before he could add anything else.

Tinacling was watching the approach from Opal. But Wes suddenly realized they were much closer to Okapogum than to Opal. And the way people thronged through this supposedly empty country . . . Back down by the ford the preacher was still warning the horses that the wages of sin is death, that wine is a mocker, and oh ye howlers . . . Wes gave the simmering venison a final glance and struck through the cottonwoods across the creek where he could see if they were about to receive visitors from the county seat and sheriff's direction.

There was a sudden splashing and the sound of galloping. As the failed preacher burst from the thicket atop the wheel horse Wes was assailed by mixed feelings. He had enough troubles now without riding herd on a madman. And the wheel horse was supernumerary—not his to begin with. As Wes watched the madman gallop off toward the county seat he guessed, on balance, he wasn't unhappy to see the poor man leave. But did the son of a bitch have to lead all the other horses off too?

CHAPTER XVII

Tinacling came running and Wes knew their disaster was complete. Then he saw the boy was not bringing more bad news, had only come to see what all the racket was. Wordlessly, the Indian watched their horses disappear in a diminishing cloud of dust. "One less for dinner," he muttered.

Wes tried to look on the bright side of it. The county seat was within easy walking distance. He had planned on making a stand here anyhow—wait for Hurley to show up from down below or for the first stranger to reveal himself on the road from Opal. But what he had not planned on was being stuck here unhorsed, with no mobility or choice left him.

Where would the preacher go? If that addlepated man knew what was good for him he wouldn't show up in Okapogum riding the stage company's horses and with a possible reputation as a labor agitator.

Tinacling studied the rapidly settling dust impassively. "Better get back," he said, and returned to the Opal side of the creek to see what new disaster came to plague their latter end. Then, as he was leaving the boy turned back to Wes. "The rifle too?" he asked.

Wes had removed the Sharps and cartridges from the boot when he dismounted. But he had also left them down near the ford lest whoever tended the fire see him first and draw obvious conclusions about an armed man in silent approach. He hastened down to where he had leaned the Sharps in the fork of a nascent cottonwood.

Studying the bent-barreled rifle, Wes knew it was his own fault. Men, in general, were hesitant to respond in this fashion to those who had saved them from suffering or possibly death. But a man of God could always justify the most outrageous behavior as the will of his God. After all, gods are not bound by the rules of human behavior.

Meditating on his sins, Wes knew he was not exactly back where he had started. A few days ago he had been penniless, unarmed, friendless, and getting on. Now he had managed to progress from this passive condition to being on the run, with several distinct sets of enemies, still penniless, unarmed, still lame, and still in the same cracked boots. Though the stew ought to be about ready, he was not really hungry any more.

He dished up a bowl and took it out where Tinacling still watched the road from Opal. "Rifle?" the boy repeated. Wes shook his head. The boy took the bowl. "For what we are about to receive, oh Lord, may we be truly thankful," he growled.

Wes had heard that phrase before from men under fire. He studied the boy at some length. "I'm sorry," he said. "You'd better cut out while you can."

"Where to?"

Wes shrugged. He studied the heat-shimmery flat that led back to Opal. Empty. "Better both cut out," he amended. "There's no use involving the old man in something he didn't ask for."

"Did you ask for it?"

"Guess I must have. In any event, I got it." They abandoned the watch and went back into the thicket. Wes dished up another bowl of stew and took it to the ancient who was still in attendance at the still. "We're leavin' now," he told the old man.

Bridges blew on his stew and ate noisily as befits a man

with few teeth. "Suit y'self," he said. "But yew know, 'tain't just me you're leavin'."

Wes knew. The girl had gotten him out of the powder magazine-jail. She had let herself be caught so he could escape. Was it all to be for nothing? "Thought you'd be happy to see the last of us," he mused.

"Might be I could wish you'd never come," Bridges said around a chunk of venison.

Wes forced himself to eat, then went to the creek and scrubbed the three telltale bowls. It was late afternoon and still no sign of pursuit from Opal. He and the boy did what they could to obliterate any trace of their presence at Bridges' place, then began working their way upstream through the cottonwoods. It had been a long day. It promised to be a longer night. What was he going to do? Go stand watch, he guessed. Tinacling looked even more used up than Wes felt.

He left the boy curled up in a thicket and wormed his way out where he could see the road from Opal. He remembered the venerable Hawken rifle the ancient had pointed at him on their first meeting. But he already knew this was no country for a man alone without a weapon. Even if Wes were to know how much powder the antique could take, he could not deprive an old man of his only friend. At the first sign, he and the boy would move still farther upstream—draw disaster away from Bridges' place.

When in doubt, act. Any movement was better than losing the initiative, letting the enemy call the shots. But, hours later, Wes still sat in the moonlight, gazing across the flat toward Opal, trying to decide what next. It was a silent night, as without wind as the day and not even the cottonwood leaves trembled. Then abruptly he heard the sound of hooves close by. Not just one horse; they were making more noise than a whole squadron of yellowlegs.

Helpless, unarmed, Wes crouched in the thicket. They were all over the place, seemingly hundreds of them, though experience told him fifteen or twenty men could create this much chaos on a raid. He heard a single shot, then heavy thumping, clanking sounds. Abruptly the smell of whiskey that hung like a miasma in the creek bottom was overpowering. There was a "whump" and flames rose.

Wes couldn't understand it. These men were not hunting for anything—not making the slightest effort to comb the underbrush where he lay watching. They seemed hell-bent on destruction. The still was ruined, done to unsalvageable bits with axes and sledgehammers. The cabin was ablaze. Where was Tinacling? Where was old Bridges?

The sons of bitches were singing, chanting. It took a while to catch the words but Wes knew the tune. He'd heard it often enough in his life:

> Onward Christian soldiers,
> Marching as to war.
> With the cross of Jesus
> Going on before.

Listening to the war chant of a militant faith, Wes suddenly knew he had not seen the last of that cracked organizer. The preacher who'd stolen their horses was behind this —working the will of an angry God against the poisoners of mankind, the allies of Demon Rum. Wes had known the man was crazy. Why hadn't he done something about it? But what? Kill him? There'd been no way to confine the stranger. If he'd only been as ruthless as that maniac was now, Wes would still be in possession of the horses and a working firearm.

And still they raged, doing in the name of God those things no civilized man dared do in his own. It wasn't that

Wes hadn't seen things like this before. He'd seen them entirely too often, but murder and mutilation in Wes's experience had always obeyed the Mosaic Law, were the logical outcome of something that began when frightened and angry soldiers had looked upon their own dead and seen what a well-honed kris or bolo can do to captured flesh.

But this was the United States. This was supposed to be civilization. What had happened to the country while he'd been gone? Or had it always been this way and he too occupied with his own affairs to pay attention?

He could understand the organizer-preacher. Madmen's minds followed their own tortured logic. But how had this stranger descended upon a small town, and how, in so short a time, had he managed to call out the worst in so many? He'd struggled to stir up a mob in Opal. And Wes had stopped him neatly and without effort. These were no saloon hangers-on. These were solid citizens—Christians!

The cabin was blazing solidly now, fed with the alcohol from still-uncut whiskey that Bridges had stored there. Even ablaze, he could smell the sweetish, dirty-old-man stink. There was another muffled "whump." A jug of booze, or had Bridges' supply of black powder for his ancient rifle gone up?

There was a faint whisper of breeze and the smoke drifted toward Wes, sickening him with the sweetish stink. Like meat burning. And then he remembered the single shot. This convocation of the godly had shot the old man in his fetid bed. Wes wondered if Bridges had managed to finish dying before the flames got to him.

But there had only been one shot. Where was Tinacling? The boy had been sleeping in the brush some distance from the cabin. With any luck he would have awoken and gotten away in time. The solid citizens were nearly finished with their rampage now. Soon, Wes suspected, the more chicken-hearted would begin to realize what they had done, that they had gone perhaps a trifle beyond the call of Christian duty. Tomorrow some of them would be afflicted with a sickness that would last the rest of their lives, whose gnawing ache could only know momentary solace while embarked upon another campaign to fulfill the need of an angry God.

The whisper of wind shifted and the sweetish stench of burning flesh drifted away until he could breathe again. He breathed deeply, struggling to contain the impotent anger that churned his stomach. Sanctimonious, hypocritical bastards! Was this the civilization he had spread through the Orient?

He remembered Tinacling's description of Hoggins up at the mine. "If he was an Indian they'd give him a fair trial and then hang him." If these illustrious citizens were to catch the boy in braids hanging around here, there wouldn't even be the interruption of a "fair trial."

The boy couldn't be over fifteen. They'd put in a rough day. Wes remembered how soundly he used to sleep at that age—before there had been any memories to keep him awake. It was possible that the boy might still be asleep, not even aware of the danger he was in. Wes tried to weigh the pros and cons. Maybe he ought to leave him alone. If he were to move out of his own hole, he might bring the whole pack of them down on the sleeping boy.

They had done about all the damage they could do here—had destroyed the still, the old man's stock in trade, his cabin, and the brief remainder of his life. What else could they do? Where in hell was Hurley? Was he up here with them? Leading them? Somehow Wes suspected he was not. Those few times he had met the sheriff that red-mustached man had seemed sensible and self-contained. Either he didn't know about this outrage or he couldn't get together enough hands to put a stop to it. It would never be easy for any small-town lawman to restrain the forces of "righteousness."

Another "whump" and a geyser of sparks as the roof of Bridges' cabin collapsed. By the time it was burnt out there would remain little of the old man: a few bones, a tooth perhaps of the half-dozen remaining him.

The shouting and singing were dying down. He hadn't heard a hallelujah for nearly a minute. Would they ever call it a night and go home?

If only there were a God . . . something created in the image of human bloodlust . . . if only a soul could survive an eternity. Eternity was not long enough to reward these crusaders in fitting fashion.

There was a rustling of leaves and crackling of underbrush. Wes stared, unable to believe the incredible luck that was bringing one of these Christians practically within reach. And the shadowy figure was not just a man of righteousness—he was also a rifle and a bandolier. Wes wondered what he was doing out here so far from the cabin wandering around in the dark, then abruptly he saw. Turned half away from him, the Christian soldier was relieving his bladder. Maybe there is a God, Wes decided.

He began moving silently. Damn! In the thrill of the chase he had nearly forgotten his bad knee. He inventoried his position, began moving again, working around that bad knee. There was still enough background noise from the burning cabin and the other men. Wes was standing now, within two paces of the man who still sprayed blithely, bathing the trunk of a cottonwood with the assiduous attention of a mongrel dog.

Wes had his belt off, was moving closer to the godly quartermaster who was about to supply him with a rifle and ammunition. He was raising the belt in his two hands when he wondered again momentarily where the boy was hiding. Surely he was awake by now.

"Here's another one of them!" It was a voice shrill with excitement, replete with righteousness. So they had found the boy—found him somewhere close at hand. Then Wes knew that it wasn't the boy they had found. Something whistled and struck him glancingly over one ear. As he felt himself spinning, falling backward and down into a funneling vortex of nothingness, Wes knew the forces of righteousness had triumphed once again.

CHAPTER XVIII

There were sounds of angry men and galloping horses and Wes wasn't sure whether he was hearing something new or remembering what had awakened him the first time. This time as he opened his eyes it was dawning and he was not alone. As he saw them looking down on him, he struggled to move and decided they must have tied him up. The faces shimmered and he sank back into unconsciousness, wondering fuzzily if the boy had managed to escape.

He was going over Niagara Falls in a leaky barrel that suddenly burst apart leaving him at the mercy of the cataract. Then, as he returned to reality, the Niagara shrank to a hatful of creek some stranger was pouring over him.

It was a possibility Wes had lived with as long as he could remember. Tempered by the knowledge of what the civilized side did to captured prisoners, he had long ago resolved never to be taken alive. But as he gasped and struggled to turn his face from the cascading water Wes knew he had failed in this, too.

Bleary eyes gave him a momentary double vision of two men, two hatfuls of water. Then two strangers coalesced into one red-mustached man and he knew it was not a stranger.

"You awake now?" Hurley asked.

Wes struggled to sit and didn't quite make it. His head was aching with a throbbing virulence even worse than after his youthful experiments with whiskey.

"You'll live," the sheriff assured him. "Can't say whether that's for better or for worse. Be damned if I didn't expect better of you."

Wes wondered what the hell he was talking about. "The boy get away?" he asked.

"What boy?"

Wes guessed that answered his question. "They killed the old man," he added.

"They?" Hurley asked. "I s'pose you're goin' t'try'n tell me you weren't in on it."

Suddenly Wes was sitting, headache forgotten. He expressed himself at length and in detail regarding the citizens who had perpetrated this outrage. "I'd sooner hook up with honest high-graders and stage robbers than with that bunch of scum!" he concluded.

The sheriff regarded him quizzically and without comment. His outburst finished, Wes's head was once more aching. He stared at the just-rising sun and wished he had a hat. Then he wondered if he would live long enough to need one. "You alone?" he asked.

"Boys rounded up a couple of them responsible citizens," Hurley said. "They'll talk." He paused and added musingly, "'Course, it won't do any good. Jury of their peers. But, by God, they're all gonna git their noses rubbed in it before this county forgets it. I don't that much care 'bout bein' sheriff any more nohow."

Wes studied the red-mustached man and concluded that he had encountered that rarest of commodities in these parts: an honest man.

"What boy?"

The boy, Wes realized, had gotten clean away. No point in involving Tinacling in it. Then he remembered that the black-braided boy had been much in evidence as they had escaped from the powder magazine-jail with Miss Upton.

"You haven't heard any news from Opal lately?" he asked.

"Not since you left with the stage."

Wes sighed. "You're going to hear it all sooner or later. Might as well get my side of it first."

"Kind of figured something was goin' on," Hurley mused when he had finished. "But I never could put my finger on it."

Wes's head still ached. Nor did it improve when he thought of Miss Upton still at the mercy of Ford and Polk up there in Opal—if she were still alive. The company bull had been hesitant to kill him openly. Perhaps he would be equally cautious about the girl.

"Not the easiest story on earth to believe," Hurley muttered.

Wes supposed it was not. Somebody might even put two and two together and conclude that he, a recently arrived stranger in this country, had cooked something up with Miss Upton before that competent young lady had appeared.

"No." Hurley did not believe that. "You say Mr. Upton knew all about you—where you come from and so on. Who d'you s'pose dug up all that information for him?"

So that was the way it was. Upton must've already suspected—or doubted the competence of his own company police. "Wish you'd warned me," he groused. "Upton might still be alive."

"So might old Bridges if you'd had your wits about you," Hurley snapped. "'Twas you let that crazy son of a bitch loose to go stir up the animals."

"Where is he?"

Hurley shrugged. "That kind only sticks around long enough to stir things up—never long enough to get caught." He paused and studied Wes. "I s'pose you know there's only one way you're goin' to make it into town alive. You ready?"

"Do I have to go?"

"What good can you do out here? I can't spare you a gun."

"What good can I do in town?"

"Offhand, I'd say you're the best bait I got."

It was nice to know that despite his failures Wes was still good for something. "Don't s'pose there's any chance of headin' back to Opal and gettin' the girl out?" he parried.

" 'Bout as much chance as a snowball in hell," Hurley agreed. "By now they'll have every mucker in town loaded for bear."

It was pointless to remark that the muckers would be misled, backing the wrong side as usual. Wes tried to stand, didn't quite make it, and allowed the sheriff to help him. Hurley got him on the spare horse, then mounted his own to tie Wes's hands to the saddle horn. They rode up out of the creek bottom, across the brief stretch of flat, and began the hair-raising descent down the sharp curves of the final drop into the county seat.

Riding single file, with the sheriff leading his horse, it was not quite so frightening as in the coach. Still, Wes would have been more at ease with his hands untied, with at least some chance to jump free of a falling horse. As they descended the hairpins he remembered how the whole town had turned out to witness the arrival of the mud wagon. How many citizens were watching this charade of the sheriff returning with a captured prisoner?

Hurley had not tied him as securely as if he might actually be trying to escape. Still, the rawhide thongs were chafing, and as the sun climbed Wes's head seemed to grow larger and more fragile. As the horses picked their nervous way down the rutted incline Wes began picking at the bonds. Might as well loosen them and get his blood circulating again. Since Hurley would be putting him in jail, it made no difference.

But with his head aching and the morning sun getting hotter, it was surprisingly difficult to concentrate. Wes considered chewing, but he knew if he were to bend over he might keep right on going.

"I s'pose you know people're watching," Hurley warned in a low voice. "Don't go makin' any sudden moves back there or givin' anybody an excuse to shoot you."

It would have been safer, Wes guessed, to have ridden in front under the eyes and gun of the sheriff. But his hands were tied and on a trail as ticklish as this the sheriff had to lead. He kept his head down and his elbows close in, trying not to make it too obvious that he was struggling with the rawhide that held his wrists to the saddle horn.

"Funny how all these things seem to come together at once," Hurley said just loud enough for Wes to hear. "Mine owners gettin' high-graded, stage gettin' robbed, then out o' nowhere a stranger comes to stir up a strike. Seems almost as if somebody was busy plannin' it all."

Wes had heard similar arguments about Creation. "You mean Ford and the Polks, or you figurin' that preacher ain't as crazy as he acts?"

"Don't know exactly what I'm thinkin'," Hurley said. "But somehow there still seems t'be something missing."

"What?"

Hurley muttered something, but Wes didn't get it. The sun was still climbing, and as it climbed Wes's head seemed to swell apace. What had those solid citizens hit him with? Whatever, he guessed he ought to be thankful the sheriff had arrived in time to break up their party. Those citizens would undoubtedly have strung him up if Hurley hadn't happened along.

And where was Tinacling? Somewhere upcreek hiding in the brush, Wes supposed. Any way he looked at it, he and the Indian boy, Miss Upton—they were all up the creek. And so was Hurley. The solid citizens of this town could vote him out—would vote him out if he tried to bring them to trial for the murder of old man Bridges. Even if the sheriff were to sacrifice himself on the altar of integrity, these citizens would serve on the jury, would turn loose any of their own. He wondered why Hurley was going as far as this? Was the sheriff truly fed up with hypocrisy and corruption?

His head was aching abominably, but still Wes struggled to understand what he had gotten into. Ford and the Polks were high-grading. Were they with the stage bandits, or was it every man for himself? The sheriff had a point. That madman of a preacher had shown up at a wondrously convenient time to stir up these already muddy waters. Coincidence? Wes had ceased believing in coincidence shortly after he had lost his faith in Santa Claus.

They were over halfway down the hill now, and he could see the citizens of the town staring up from whatever patches of shade the main and only street afforded. Chances were there would be at least one pair of field glasses among them. He gave up the struggle with the rawhide that held him to the saddle. It was pointless. They would be in town in another five minutes and Hurley would cut him loose.

And then what? Bait for the sheriff's trap? Wes suspected there were facets to this situation that he had still to see. If only his head weren't aching so bad. . . . He would sit in jail, and unless the sheriff's men had already put a crimp into those citizens, somebody would probably be organizing a necktie party. It finally occurred to Wes that surrendering might not have been the smartest thing he ever did. But what choice had he? If he'd resisted Hurley could have brought him in easily enough anyway.

Citizens in jail. Possibly one of them would be the man who had rapped him over the ear. Wes breathed deeply and tried to make the sun stop jiggling up and down with each movement of the plodding horse. Hurley, he decided, was up to something else. The sheriff probably hadn't lied to him. Neither had he told Wes the whole truth.

"You gonna put me in the same cell with all those Christian soldiers?" Wes asked.

"Shut up," the sheriff explained.

Wes squinted into two jiggling suns and saw the time was past for any private communication with his captor. They were on the final stretch—where he had stopped to untie the mud wagon's rear wheels. They were within earshot of the silent waiting town. It couldn't be more than eight in the morning and already the sun was pounding on Wes's bare head, driving him down like a tent stake.

Within minutes he would be out of the sun—safe in jail where he could lie down and relax and hope his head would stop aching. His plodding horse stumbled and Wes nearly pitched from the saddle. If he were to fall, he would still hang from the horn by his bound hands. It would spook the horse and he might travel quite a distance in that ungainly fashion before something came loose. Wes took a deep breath, held it, gritted his teeth, and concentrated on hanging on until they could make the cool shade of the jail.

His flat-heeled infantryman's boots were not made for riding. He let himself slouch toward the stiff-kneed side, counting on that rigid leg to hold him upright. "Hurry up," he managed through gritted teeth. "Hurry. I'm startin' to come apart."

Hurley half turned in the saddle and started to say something. But at that minute the shooting started.

CHAPTER XIX

His luck, Wes decided, had finally run out. Light-headed, tied to his horse, he was going to be shot down in plain sight. But there was nothing like approaching death to clear a man's head and focus his attention. Through suddenly clear eyes he saw the staring citizens were as startled as he was.

There had only been two shots. Neither of them had hit Wes. But as the man in front of him spun and fell from the saddle, Wes knew the sheriff had taken at least one hit. People were still staring awestruck, just beginning to look for where the shots had come from when Hurley finished falling from the saddle. A third bullet shrieked past Wes, missing him but creasing his horse's rump. The horse reared and its reins whipped free from the falling sheriff's grasp. Then both horses had turned and were galloping back uphill.

Wes hung on, knowing his life depended on it. It was hopeless any way. There was close to a mile of switchback road folded compactly into five hundred vertical feet of hairpins, all in plain sight of the town. Anybody able to hit Hurley could pick Wes off at leisure as his horse climbed that hill. And how long before the horse's panic was worked out of him by that merciless climb? He was barely to the first switchback, reins dragging when Wes heard the rising roar of voices behind him.

The sheriff's riderless horse bolted past, nearly forcing Wes's over the bank. There was a shot and the animal screamed with renewed panic, drawing a fresh burst of speed as Wes's beast strove to follow. Wes struggled to stay on the horse, fought to untie Hurley's rawhide, cursed himself for not working harder at it while he'd had a chance.

Hurley hadn't tied the knots all that tight. They were mostly for show. But still they were more than Wes could manage by himself. The rawhide was slick now and he guessed he was sweating, then saw his wrists were bleeding. It was now or never, he decided, and gave his all in a single skin-peeling jerk. The sight of his skinned and bloody wrist would sicken him if he had time to be sick but—his hand was free. He shook his other hand out of the now loose thongs and leaned over the horse's neck to capture the reins. One low-heeled infantryman's boot went through the stirrup.

He was hanging by one hand and by his good leg, the stirrup drawn up on top of the saddle. A bullet whizzed through where he would have been if he'd been sitting properly instead of playing these hazardous games. Another bullet came and his foot was numb with sudden shock. Hang here another second and he would never have the strength to get back up. He heaved mightily and felt himself scoot back up atop the horse. His good foot was numb, but at least it was still in the stirrup. He lay forward over the horn, gripping horn and reins with his left hand while he struggled to work the stirrup back down the bleeding shin of his stiff leg. The horse swung round another switchback, still following its riderless companion, who now galloped a hundred yards ahead.

Finally Wes got the stirrup back down past the heel of his boot. There were more shots now but they were not coming as close. He risked a glance down at his good foot, wondering if he would ever walk again. It was still numb with shock. Then he saw what had happened. A bullet had torn the wornout heel from his boot. As if he didn't have enough trouble not slipping through these stirrups!

It was like those toy animals that paraded back and forth in shooting galleries. At the switchbacks he was fairly safe but the central stretch of each run was a clear straight shot from the town below. The only thing that had saved his life so far, Wes suspected, was that they were shooting practically straight up. If one of these hunters were to start leading like somebody shotgunning birds instead of aiming rifle style, Wes knew he might never make it. But as he squinted past the flowing mane of his mount he could see he must be at least halfway up.

The horse was drenched with sweat, flanks heaving, every rasping breath drifting back to drench Wes with slobber. He wondered which would give out first—himself or the horse. They passed the shooting gallery section and rounded another switchback and then he was bending low over the horse's mane again. There was a shot and a horse screamed. But not his horse. Were the citizens so excited they couldn't even tell which horse he was riding?

Maybe not. They were shooting up and he was already so high he must be practically invisible from their angle. But his horse wouldn't stay spooked forever. The horse was ready to drop now. And surely there were other horses in town. There had been plenty of them last night when they had come to burn out the old man. By now some of them would be saddled up and on their way after him.

Or would those chicken-hearted murderers . . . ?

His headache was gone now. Sooner or later it would be back with interest, Wes knew. But for now he was thinking clearly, seeing how it would look from the eyewitness point of view. The sheriff had been riding into town leading Wes's horse, with Wes naturally behind. Fully nine out of ten of those eyewitnesses would be willing to swear the prisoner had somehow gotten hold of a hidden gun and had gunned down the sheriff right in front of everybody!

The rib-heaving horse rounded another switchback and started up another shooting gallery straightaway. Wes had to kick his unspurred heels and encourage the horse like a platoon of reluctant infantrymen. This time he could hear the whizzing of bullets a second before the pop. How many more turns? The riderless sheriff's mount had disappeared somewhere up ahead. Wes yelled and kicked his sweat-spraying horse around another switchback, bracing himself for another trip across the shooting gallery when abruptly he realized he was off the face of the cliff—up on the flat. He gave a final glance down toward town where horses and men were beginning to appear, then urged his heaving horse onward at a fast walk. If he were to let the horse stand now he feared it might never move again.

By the time he had walked the horse to the creek and the ashes of Bridges' cabin the animal had cooled out. Still no pursuit had topped the rise. Wes gave a sour laugh. They had been good at murdering an old man in his sleep. But by now they would have convinced themselves that Wes was armed to the teeth and it would require endless hunting for more armament, more strategy if a score of citizens were to capture one unarmed fugitive on a spent horse.

While the cooled-out horse drank, Wes washed the blood from his skinned wrist and hand. He wanted to wash the bloody mass of hair above his ear but every time he touched it he felt dizzy again.

That damned horse was going to drink too much. Wes forced him away from the water and struggled to mount. He was aching—not just in the head, but in every joint and fissure of his abused body. But he couldn't stay here.

There was an owl hoot. *In midmorning?* Wes listened

and the sound repeated. "Tinacling?" he called softly. "You around here anywhere?"

Clean-faced, hair freshly washed and braided, the boy emerged from the cottonwood undergrowth. "Let me have the horse," he urged.

"Why?"

"Because you're too banged up to do it."

"Do what?"

"Catch that other horse," the boy said with a trace of impatience. "The bay that tore through here ten minutes ago with saddle, bridle, everything but a sheriff on its back."

"Oh," Wes said. Exhaustion was catching up with him. He watched the boy urge his tired horse away upstream then, with a glance behind, began working his way deeper into the cottonwoods. Dimly he realized that this attractive shade and moisture would not be his alone. All he needed now was some territorial dispute with a rattler. But he made it without incident and found room to lie down—hopefully without tracks. His headache had returned with compound interest, aggravated now by a stirrup-skinned shin and the stinging of his lacerated wrist. But . . . he was alive. From the heavy way the sheriff had fallen, he was pretty sure Hurley was not.

Sore and aching as he was, Wes didn't exactly sleep but he sank into a comatose semiconsciousness and lost track of time. When he came to with a jerk the boy squatted on his heels watching him. "How'd you find me?" Wes mumbled.

Tinacling gave him an odd look and Wes guessed he hadn't been as thorough as he'd thought about covering his trail. "Half-dozen hard cases rode up from town and poked through the ashes for a while before they went back," the boy said. "Did you really kill the sheriff?"

Wes shook his head and immediately wished he hadn't. "Figured you'd be long gone by now," he said.

The boy shrugged. "Gone where? Sooner or later everybody has to pass by here. And speaking of which—" The boy broke off to disappear for a moment. Wes was still getting to his feet and struggling to get his broken head together when the boy returned. "They'll be here in a quarter of an hour."

"Who?"

"One man and one horse coming across the flat from Opal. First sign of anybody from that direction."

Now that was interesting. Why had they waited so long? Wes could make a fair guess. With neither telephone nor telegraph and thanks to Miss Upton's delaying tactic, he and the boy had gotten clean away. Ford and Polk would have known Wes could either get clean away—or do his damage in the county seat. Which in turn meant they had not had Hurley in their pocket or they wouldn't have stayed holed up in Opal all this time dithering. But when neither sheriff nor posse appeared in Opal, the company bull must have decided Wes was too scared to waste time sounding out the sheriff. If he had slipped through town without stopping, it was time for them to present an official version of how and by whom Upton had been murdered.

"Did you catch the horse?" Wes asked.

Tinacling shook his head. "Didn't catch the carbine in that saddle boot either."

The horse Wes had ridden was tethered upstream from the ashes of Bridges' cabin. If he ever found time—if he lived long enough, Wes resolved to poke through the ashes and give the ancient's remains a decent burial. But meanwhile . . .

They moved back through the cottonwoods to the ford and made what preparations the unarmed and walking wounded can make against an armed and presumably alert man. Wes wondered if whoever was coming would know Bridges had lived near here.

From where he waited crouched in the fork of a cottonwood Wes couldn't see too well. He squinted and listened, waiting for the stranger to work his way across the heatshimmery flat. Finally man and horse hove into view, sweating profusely, though they moved only at a walk.

From somewhere near him there was a faint rustle in the cottonwood thicket. Tinacling, Wes supposed. His stirrupbarked shin was throbbing most ungodly and Wes began to worry about blood poisoning. The mass of hair and scab above his ear seemed slightly larger than before. He was still having trouble with his vision, seeing double unless he squinted and forced himself to concentrate. He was not in the best shape to mount an ambush. But if he muffed this chance, would he ever get another?

Man and horse drew nearer and he abruptly recognized the roan leader the girl had been riding during their abortive escape. He wondered if the horse would go smelling him and doglike, give their position away. But the roan plodded dispiritedly, as if it had been a long time between feedings. The horse didn't even pick up speed as it neared the cool, flowing water of the ford.

Wes squinted, trying to make out the unfamiliar figure in bottle-green shirt and floppy straw hat that covered most of his face. Whoever he was, the man was no more of a horseman than was Wes. He bounced miserably atop the plodding lead horse, matching himself to the gait with all the grace and skill of a sack of potatoes.

But if he was not a horseman, at least the stranger was a gunman. He carried a carbine of some sort in a saddle boot. There was a pistol high on his left side, belted backward for a cross draw. Horse and man plodded closer and then Wes could see beneath the shade of the floppy straw hat. For a tiny instant Wes wondered if he had been mistaken. Perhaps there really was a God after all. The man approaching the ford was the green-eyeshaded stage agent—the man who had watched Ford shoot the mine manager. Wes drew a deep breath and held it.

CHAPTER XX

He was in the fork of a cottonwood directly above the stream where old Bridges had drawn down on him. Presumably any man or horse would stop to drink here after the dusty dryness of the road from Opal.

Any man . . . but the creature aboard the horse was of a lesser breed. It was hard to understand why he was so frightened. Surely he wouldn't be making this trip unless they were sure Wes was long gone. Yet the stage agent in floppy straw hat was approaching the ford with all the eagerness of a kid nearing a graveyard on a foggy night. He was twisting his neck, searching the cottonwood thickets to each side of the narrow roadway until Wes was sure he must have been spotted.

The tired horse wanted to stop and drink, but Green Eyeshade snarled and spurred until the horse moved reluctantly on. Damn! Wes was still not thinking well—had used most of his remaining energy just in climbing this tree. Horse and rider passed beneath him, were nearly beyond range before he realized they would not stop, that his only chance was moving inexorably on and away. He sprang, praying that as they came off the horse he would manage to land on top. Then a lariat streaked from the opposite side of the ford and settled over Green Eyeshade's shoulders. Wes was committed, already flying through the air. He hit the station agent an instant after the rope and they tumbled off the horse. To Wes's mild surprise the horse didn't spook—

only ambled off another couple of paces and began drinking.

The station agent was livid with terror, unable to speak, even if the wind hadn't been knocked out of him. Tinacling appeared and matter-of-factly tossed the other end of the lariat over a high branch. Wes tried not to show his wear and tear. He adjusted the noose upward until it fit neatly around Green Eyeshade's neck. The boy bound the station agent's nerveless hands behind his back and adjusted tension on the lariat until the short man was standing on tiptoes.

Leaving him thus to meditate on his sins, they went their separate ways, Wes to secure the horse and carbine, the boy to make sure no surprises were coming from the county seat. Horse tied and carbine handy, Wes removed the gun and belt from the man who stood on tiptoe, sweating and breathing himself into panicky hyperventilation.

The revolver was a new 1899 model Smith and Wesson thirty-eight. Wes swung the cylinder out and noted approvingly that it was new, clean, with untarnished ammunition. He removed his belt to put on the gun, then changed his mind and peeled Green Eyeshade's pants off too. They would end on Wes at midcalf, but at a distance it wouldn't matter. He unbuttoned Polk's bottle-green shirt and donned it too.

The carbine was an 1895 Marlin chambered to carry nine 45–90 cartridges. "Huntin' elephants?" Wes asked. "I sure could've used a gun like this when I was drivin' stage."

Polk was not amused. His mouth worked several times and finally he chittered, "What're you goin' t'do t'me?"

"Depends," Wes said. "How's Miss Upton's health these days?"

Tinacling returned from checking out the road to the

county seat. He glanced at Wes, then began solemnly piling firewood around the naked stage agent's bare tiptoes.

"Not the dry stuff like that," Wes cautioned. "Green. We want a *slooooooow* fire."

"The girl's fine," the stage agent managed in a shrill voice. "Why would anybody want to kill her?"

"Don't know," Wes said. "Why would anybody want to kill Mr. Upton?"

"That's different."

"Oh?" Wes waited. When Polk remained silent, he nodded at Tinacling who solemnly returned to gathering firewood.

"Got a dull knife?" the boy asked.

"What you need it for?"

"Us savages," the boy said. "You'll have to indulge our quaint tribal customs."

"Off in the saddlebag," Wes said, pointing toward a nonexistent commissary. When the boy had disappeared he turned to Polk. "Sorry about this," he said in a confidential voice. "If you was to talk fast though, maybe I could get him to just shoot you instead of, uh—"

"But you're a white man!" Polk wailed.

"Right," Wes said with an air of sudden resolve. "No use waitin' for him to come back. I'll do it myself." He raised the Smith and Wesson, began squeezing the trigger, changed his mind. "Too light a bullet," he said, and picked up the carbine. "This'n'll blow you right in two. Never know what hit you." He aimed at Polk's face, took his time, wiped his eyes several times, checked the rifle and shook his head. "Might miss," he said. "Mind if I try for a bigger target?" He aimed at the stage agent's naked belly and began squeezing again.

"No you don't!" Tinacling yelled gleefully from behind the unhappy Polk. He stretched and gathered a handful of straggly hair together before beginning a semicircular scratch around the stage agent's bald spot with a broken twig. Polk gave a soprano shriek and fainted.

"Funny," Tinacling muttered. "He thought it was funny when they did that to me."

They left Polk to his own devices for a moment to check the road out both ways. When they returned the small man's face was rapidly turning blue. The boy untied the lariat and lowered him part way. Wes splashed water until he was breathing regularly.

Finally Green Eyeshade could talk again. "What do you want to know?" he asked.

"Your mother's middle name. And after that we'll have to go into detail," Wes said.

While Tinacling made periodic checks on the approaches to the ford, Wes garnered the details of what the Polks and that other Ford had been up to. He was mildly satisfied to discover that he hadn't been wrong on any of the important points. Hurley hadn't been in on it. Much good would that do the dead sheriff now.

Neither had the bandits been in on it at first. Then after learning how much they were supposed to have taken and comparing it with the paltry amount they had actually gotten from the strongbox, the bandits had approached Ford and cut themselves in on the high-grading operation. Things had gone along smoothly enough until Polk had decided it was pointless to share all this wealth with men born to be hung— especially when they could just as easily be blamed for it and never get it. That had been one holdup before Wes had been hired to serve as clay pigeon.

"And who are the bandits?" Wes demanded.

Polk's normal air of snappish impatience was returning by degrees as he began to suspect he might not die immediately. "You killed a couple of brothers. Claymore, Clayton–Clay something or other. Hurley'll know."

Not any more, he won't. "And the others?"

"Seems like there was a Gibbons among them. Round up any one and Hurley'll squeeze the rest of the names out of him just like—like you squeezed me," the little man finished lamely. Wes decided to let it go at that.

"You gonna keep me hangin' here forever?" Polk complained.

"I dunno. Depends on what you can tell me about Miss Upton."

The small man looked at Wes as if he wasn't quite all there. "Why would anybody want to harm her?"

Why indeed? Wes regarded him in silence.

"I knew it!" Polk triumphed. "I knew there was something funny that day she got away from you. You turned her loose, didn't you—just to slow us down."

"Something like that," Wes agreed.

Behind Polk, Tinacling was studying Wes, his face as expressionless as a Fenimore Cooper Indian's. Wes stared back at the boy searching for inspiration. He had verified a few suspicions. He was still not out of the woods. Now that Hurley was dead, who was the law down in the county seat? If it was one of those Christian soldiers who'd been up here last night . . .

Silently, the boy got to his feet and went once more to check the approaches to the ford. In a moment he came back with his finger to his lips. Wes checked his ammunition and scooted off into the brush where he could watch the naked station agent. Tinacling mounted the saddled horse and moved out again. There was a brief sound of hooves galloping and moments later the boy returned leading the horse Hurley had been riding.

So once more they had enough horses to go around.

Arms too. Wes had Polk's carbine and revolver. Now the
boy had Hurley's carbine. None of which would be enough
for them to make it down the shooting-gallery switchbacks
from here to the county seat. And . . . even if they were to
make it, what would they do once they got there?

His one contact with sane, law-abiding citizenry in this
region had been Hurley. With the sheriff dead, with Upton
dead, with the girl in a parlous position where she dared not
reveal what she knew . . . The boy seemed to be reading
Wes's mind. "Why don't we just kill this sniveling son of a
bitch and leave?" he suggested. "Let them sort it out for
themselves?"

"I've told you everything I know!" Polk wailed, once
more in a panic.

Looking past the stage agent's naked shoulder, Wes saw
that even as he said it Tinacling remembered the girl. They
couldn't leave her in this position for, capable as she might
appear, Miss Upton was totally vulnerable in a male-
dominated society.

Was it the knock he'd taken on the head? Wes still
couldn't figure out what to do. He studied the naked stage
agent and tried to get his thoughts in order. Surely there
was something he could do. He reminded himself of the way
he had always tackled seemingly impossible tasks in the
army: Break them down into simple steps and do the easiest
thing first. By the time that was finished often Wes's subcon-
scious would have worked out some way to do the more
difficult parts of the problem. Musingly, he untied the other
end of the lariat and the station agent promptly collapsed.

When the gun Wes still pointed at him didn't go off, Polk
pulled himself together enough to put on the grimy rags
Wes had taken off. Wes motioned Polk to his feet and
herded the bedraggled man toward the ashes of Bridges'
cabin. Pointing to a shovel, Wes told him where to dig.

"Why?" Tinacling asked poutingly. "There won't be enough left to bury when I'm through with him."

Wes wondered if the boy was just talking for effect or if he had forgotten there was somebody else needed burial here. He left Polk digging under the boy's eye and began poking through the ashes of the old man's cabin.

The sod roof had collapsed almost in one piece. Wes studied the ashy outlines, oriented himself from the still-standing chimney, and began lifting sod in the corner where there had been a sodden pile of blankets. Despite the flames, there were still bits of blanket left unburnt. By now he should have uncovered something else. Had his nose quit working too?

Puzzled, Wes convinced himself that nobody had died amid those scorched blankets. He began going methodically over the rest of the cabin, lifting sods and tossing them beyond the ashes. In the middle of the cabin he found three bones with bits of meat. But even as he held them up Wes knew these were not human bones. He remembered the quarter of venison the old man had hung above the fly line. It was not in its tree.

Nor was Bridges' body in his cabin. Studying the scorched bones, Wes knew now what he had smelled the night of the fire. But if they hadn't killed old Bridges in his sleep, what had they done with the old man?

Could those Christian soldiers be less villainous than Wes had thought? Had they contented themselves with burning the old man's cabin and destroying his still? Or was Bridges feeding buzzards somewhere else on this flat?

Either way, it was pointless to keep the little stage agent digging. But . . . Wes reminded himself that the little man in the green eyeshade was an accessory to murder, and had lent his enthusiastic cooperation to laying the blame on

Wes. It would be good for his soul to spend a few more hours digging.

But where was Bridges? Then Wes glanced up from the ashes to see the grizzled ancient in greasy buckskins, leaning on his venerable Hawken as he studied them from the underbrush to one side of the burned-out cabin.

"Somebody die?" Bridges asked. "Or is somebody goin' to?"

CHAPTER XXI

"Where the hell have you been?" Wes demanded. "All them Christian soldiers throwin' a party and you weren't even there?"

It was Polk's first inkling that the grave he had been digging had not been his own. He stared at the old man with bleary unbelief.

"Been out seein' the country," Bridges cackled. Wes wondered if he was quite all there. Wes knew he had not been that cheerful when he saw his tent shredded and his homestead wrecked.

"Shore a lot of funny things goin' on around here," Bridges mused. "Even see'd one o' them fellers used to rob the stage."

There couldn't be too many of them left, Wes suspected. But there had still been four horses waiting the day he and the boy and Miss Upton had made their frantic dash from Opal.

"You may not know it," Bridges cackled, "but you saved a couple of boys' lives and made an old woman happy."

Wes wondered how he had found time to do all that.

"They 'uz down to the last two men," Bridges said. "And Jase Gibbons knew he wasn't goin' to rob no stage thataway. So ol' Jase, he went around huntin' young blood an' he stopped at the Padley place and he went and sweet-talked ol' Miz Padley's boys into goin' on the owlhoot." Bridges cackled in high glee.

"There they was astandin' alongside the road a-waitin' and you had to go'n give Jase Gibbons a case o' lead poisonin' afore they saw ary a stage. Last I heard them boys 'us in the back yard asplittin' wood and dang near ready to turn Christian."

Tinacling was amused. "Didn't any of them have a rifle?"

Wes hoped they wouldn't carry their conversion to extremes. He tried to work out how many stage robbers he had accounted for by now. Three at least. Maybe five. And Miss Upton had marked up one of them pretty good with a whip. Considering that Ford and the Polks had been getting all the real money while the bandits collected little apart from the blame, Wes could see how the temptation to go into another line of business might be overwhelming.

"Been somewheres else," the old man cackled. "Man my age takes a mind to it he can be a great walker." He paused and sniffed the heavy air among the cottonwoods. "Don't s'pose those solid citizens left a drop of anythin'?" he said wistfully.

"It's possible," Wes said. "Unless you kept it all inside the cabin. Where else'd you go?"

"Opal," Bridges said. "Took me a walk up t'Opal."

Very slowly and carefully, Polk was starting to slither up out of the half-dug grave. Tinacling guided him back into the hole with a jab of his carbine muzzle. "What's happening in Opal?" the boy asked. "The mine gone broke yet?"

"Mine's doin' great," Bridges said. "Seems like they made a big new strike."

Made it some months ago, Wes suspected. Only now that the manager and chief stockholder was dead there was no more point in trying to conceal it. He remembered the man he had surprised in total darkness the day of the cave-in. Somebody had been high-grading.

"But that ain't the big news," Bridges cackled. "Big news is Miss Alberdeen."

Wes waited, wondering what that capable young woman was up to now. Whatever it was, he suspected he was not going to like it.

"Goin' t'be a wedding." Bridges cackled in vast amusement. "Miss Upton's gettin' married to her childhood sweetheart."

Now who the hell would that be, Wes wondered sourly.

In answer to his unasked question, Bridges dropped his final bit of news. "Bet you know the lucky man. 'F you don't, leastways he does." Bridges pointed at Polk who was back in the half-dug grave.

And quite abruptly Polk was not trying to sneak out of the hole. He seemed to be shrinking, struggling to make himself invisible.

Wes studied the stage agent, shaking his head. "And here I went out of my way to promise you a nice quick easeful death," he mourned. "You just can't trust nobody no more."

"Where'd you say that dull knife was?" Tinacling asked.

"You don't skin a pig," Wes said. "You scald him."

"Might be I could patch up one o' them mash tubs," Bridges contributed.

"Him or Ford?" Wes asked the old man.

"I was goin' down to the county seat to get the preacher," Polk volunteered. "It was Ford popped the question."

Wes shook his head, midway between disbelief and exasperation. "In this day and age!" he growled. And yet he knew the derby-hatted company bull might get away with it —could still get away with it if he had the local law and a preacher in his hip pocket. And a wife could not testify against her husband . . .

"What do we do?" Tinacling asked.

At last Wes was free of this dithering indecision. Not through any virtue of his own, he guessed. The decision had been made for him. That shooting-gallery stretch of road down to Okapogum was as unrewarding as it was dangerous. And back in the hills Miss Upton was in need of a friend. "Let's get our guest here on a horse," he said, pointing at Polk.

"Well dew tell," Bridges marveled.

"You're welcome to go along if you feel like gettin' shot at again," Wes invited.

"I'd a damn sight ruther ride down to Okapogum on one o' them horses of your'n an' talk to Hurley about what them citizens did."

"You'd ruther," Wes said witheringly. "Don't look t'me like they even shot at you."

"They ain't got no call burnin' down my cabin," Bridges grumped.

"Ain't gonna do you no use to go looking for Hurley," Wes explained. "One of those solid citizens murdered him." He paused, realizing abruptly that now he was wanted for two murders.

"Funny how you're alluz around jus' when somebody's about to go git hisself kilt," Bridges mused.

Wes had meditated on that subject. "They're layin' this one onto me, too," he said.

"Are we going or staying?" Tinacling demanded. "I haven't eaten for a while and he's too greasy to be appetizing."

Polk obviously did not enjoy being talked about this way —least of all by Indians. He was pumping up his courage for another round of nastiness when abruptly he realized he was still in no position to antagonize anyone.

"Maybe I ought to shoot you," Wes said musingly. "Save you all those months of misery waitin' to find out whether they're goin' to lynch you or just hang you legally." But it would be smarter to get out of here before those citizens in Okapogum . . .

Within minutes they were on their way, Polk riding in the middle with his hands bound to the horn as Wes's had been on the ride down to Okapogum. Wearing the short man's britches, which were too loose at the waist and too short in the leg, Wes sat the same horse Hurley had furnished him. The beast seemed no worse for its frantic stampede up the shooting gallery. Bridges brought up the rear, balancing the Hawken across his saddle.

"S'pose we ought to've waited till morning," Tinacling said, eyeing the sun. It was the hottest part of the afternoon.

Wes was inclined to agree. But he remembered how easily the addlepated organizer had slipped away from them. He had no intention of seeing the stage agent perform a similar disappearing act. The short man was sweating profusely, soaking the back of Wes's ruined shirt. Hours later when the sun was down and the moon not up the man was still sweating by the brilliant starlight. Still they rode on until the horses heard yet another rattler coming out to drink and turned obstinate.

They got Polk off the horse and made sure he was not going for a stroll in the starlight—which was not too difficult since the station agent seemed as terrified at the prospect of stepping on a rattler as he was of everything else in his suddenly turbulent life.

"You planning on making town in dark or daylight?"

Wes didn't know. Either way was risky. He wondered how many guns Ford had lining the streets. Poor suckers . . . how could they know they were on the wrong side? "Daylight," he guessed. He was hungry already and nothing would be gained by growing hungrier.

They sat quietly, taking care not to wander beyond the confine of bare ground that Tinacling had swept with a lariat. Wes was still aching in every joint. The knobby mass of blood and hair over his ear ached unabated and his wrist was smarting enough to cancel any hope of sleep. One by one the others dropped off—even Polk. Wes sat listening to the distant sounds of coyotes, the closer sounds of horses, and the still closer sound of a nervous rattlesnake. He sat very quiet, hoping the snake would not cripple one of the horses.

Finally there was enough daylight to ride. They got under way again, moving with all the brisk enthusiasm of a forewarned light brigade. Polk seemed to have aged several years overnight and was still sweating despite the cool morning air. They rode in grumpy silence for another couple of hours, and then the horses were struggling to drink at the brown-foamed creek that divided Opal's single street.

They urged the horses away from the poisoned water and studied the awakening town. A whistle shrieked up at the headframe and the streets filled with a shift change. Still, they waited in the morning sunlight, horses champing nervously among the odd-angled houses of Opal's low-rent district. "I think," Wes said thoughtfully, "that Mr. Polk ought to lead the way." He turned to Bridges who seemed neither better nor worse after losing his home and spending his days under less than ideal circumstances. "Might look nice if you were in the rear," he ventured.

Bridges nodded. "Think it'll work?"

Wes didn't know. He just couldn't think of anything that would work any better. The shift change crowd had thinned out by now as the more decorous went home to bathe and sleep. But the saloons were still doing a swinging-door business as the four of them rode into town, Polk in the lead, Wes behind him, the Indian boy next and Bridges bringing up the rear with the ancient Hawken across his saddle bow. Wes and Tinacling kept their hands together on saddle horns. Up ahead Polk was still sweating buckets. "Hot," he complained. "Can't I take this shirt off?"

"Not unless I untie your hands first," Wes said in a conversational murmur. "And I'm too busy actin' like mine're tied for any shenanigans like that."

"But he'll kill me!" Polk wailed.

"Can't tell," Wes said from inside Polk's ill-fitting bottle-green shirt and calf-length trousers. "Can't really tell which of us he'll figure is most worth shuttin' up."

He had wondered how aware the average resident of Opal might be of what was actually going on. As the streets suddenly emptied at the appearance of these four horsemen, Wes knew his question was answered. "Got any idea where he'll be?" the boy asked.

Wes had an idea, but he wasn't betting on it. Slowly the four walked their horses up the single street, past the boardinghouse where Wes had shuffled a planted gold brick from beneath his bed and back into the company bull's room. They walked their horses past Yee Wing's where a pigtailed man of indeterminate age stared blankly from a doorway for a moment before unhurriedly closing it.

"It's me, Polk!" the short man began shrieking. "For God's sake don't shoot! It's me. It's meeee!" His thin voice rose to a soprano in the morning air. Those few muckers still on the street hastily disappeared. Up by the headframe, Wes could hear the clank of bells and the chuff of the hoisting engine.

"Want me to check the stage depot?" Tinacling asked.

"Don't think so," Wes said. Then he realized it might be the safest place for the boy. "Might as well," he amended. The boy was disappearing through the false-front archway when the shot came.

It was a single shot from something slow and heavy like a Sharps, and it hit Polk like a sledgehammer, knocking him backward over the cantle. He hung twitching from the side of the horse, hands still bound to the saddle horn. He died wearing Wes's clothes.

CHAPTER XXII

Of all the lousy luck! He had been riding up the single street of this town expecting exactly what had happened, with his eyes peeled and ready. And for one tiny instant he had let his eyes follow Tinacling into the stage company yard and that had to be the exact second when it happened.

The dead station agent's horse did not take kindly to all that weight hanging from one side, wrenching cinch and skin sideways. He bucked tentatively, squeezing a final wheezing groan from the man who hung by his bound hands from the horn. Wes remembered how close he had come to being in that same position as he traversed the shooting-gallery straightaways of the climb up out of Oka-pogum. But at least the short man had died quickly. Would Wes be as lucky?

He knew the shot had come from somewhere uphill and ahead of them—knew it from the way Polk had gone flying backward out of the saddle, held to the horse only by his bound hands. If Ford had been successful in making the Opal muckers believe he was on the side of the angels, then this was it. Wes could never hold out against the whole town.

He wished to Christ he'd never thought of this crazy idea. Surely if he'd taken a couple of weeks to think it over he could have come up with some kind of a less harebrained plan. If only he had two weeks. If only the girl had two weeks. But she had given hers away for him. He had to do something. He reminded himself that it would do the girl no good for him to die a noble death. And all the time he dithered like this, less than half a second had passed. The dead man's horse bucked again, failed to dislodge that cumbersome lopsided weight, and went galloping off uphill.

So here, exposed on the single street with no place to duck was no place to try to figure it out. Bridges was already in motion, charging straight uphill with a yell like Wes hadn't heard since the Philippines. Wes yelled and kicked spurless heels and got his horse moving too. Up ahead was the headframe and the shed where once he had studied mine plans with Upton. Much closer was the house-office where Miss Upton lived, where she had fed him on his first night in town.

Abruptly, Wes reined up under the eaves of the Upton home-office and slid from his horse. Bridges was still charging uphill toward the headframe. Had he seen something Wes hadn't? A shot from directly over his head nearly jarred Wes's eye teeth loose. Bridges' horse scampered for an instant, then picked up his gait again. The old man disappeared around a pile of stulls near the headframe—that pile of stulls where the cracked preacher had tried to stir up the animals.

Wes's ears were ringing and for an instant he thought he'd been shot. He moved along the narrow side walkway that led to the Upton living quarters, hugging the wall and ducking beneath the single tiny window. Upstairs glass tinkled and a piece fell on him. Now I've had it, Wes decided. Then as an octagonal Winchester barrel aimed overhead, Wes saw it was not aiming at him.

So Ford had moved into the Upton house. Wes tried not to think about what this might mean. Unwillingly he remembered a satirical song to the effect that "Heaven Will Protect the Working Girl." He was supposed to be Miss Upton's protector. Instead, she had sacrificed herself so that he could get away. Crouched in the narrow passageway, he could not see what the octagonal barreled Winchester was aiming at. He had left his carbine in the boot. He removed Polk's Smith and Wesson from the cross-draw holster and held his breath.

The Winchester fired. Down in this slot it nearly deafened Wes. He waited while the barrel withdrew slightly into the broken upstairs window to jack in a shell. The barrel came back out the window again. But not far enough. Where was the girl? Still alive, he guessed. She would have to stay alive at least long enough for a valid marriage ceremony if Ford were to be assured of profiting from all his deviltry.

Wes moved slightly and still he could not get a sight of who held the rifle. A piece of broken windowpane crunched beneath his heelless boot and he held his breath. But the blast of the Winchester must have left Ford as deaf as Wes was. He bent again, performing his awkward stiff-kneed bow to pick up a shard of glass. On his feet again, he tossed it up through the window.

That brought the company bull's puffy face out the window. The rifle aimed at Wes. Wes and Ford fired at the same instant. Even as he fired Wes knew he had missed. His bullet struck the Winchester's stock, shattering it and throwing splinters. The heavier rifle slug burned a searing line down the left side of his chest, just forward enough to avoid tearing his arm off. There was an odd thumping sound inside the room upstairs.

The Winchester was out of action, but surely Ford would have more than one weapon. Wes tried to remember where the back door was—realized he didn't know. He had only been in the house twice and each time he had entered via the front door and office.

He raced out of the passageway and around to the back of the house and there was a door. With death on the other side of it. His hearing was coming back slowly and he could still hear that odd rhythmic thumping somewhere inside the house. His left side was hurting and he didn't know how much damage the bullet had done. But he didn't dare impair his right arm. He launched himself at the door, hit it with his left shoulder and—bounced back.

The door was much solider than Wes. From the way his ribs were hurting he guessed his own damage couldn't be all that bad. After all the racket he'd made bouncing off the door there was no hope of surprise. He fired a round into the lock, knowing from bitter experience in another part of the world that this expedient seldom worked. But the back door of the Upton house was not of hardwood nor was it in the massive sixteenth-century Spanish style of other doors he had assaulted. When he tried it the door swung open.

Damn, how his wrist was smarting where he had skinned it getting out of rawhide! He balanced the S&W, trying to remember how many shots he had left. Had he only fired two? There was nobody in the kitchen. Upstairs he could still hear that rhythmic thumping. What on earth was Ford up to? Where was the girl?

Wes did his stiff-legged best up the stairs, expecting a bullet at any moment. But Ford wouldn't come down and he couldn't wait down here forever. He was upstairs and in a narrow hallway. There were two doors. One was open and it was on the wrong side of the house anyway. He gave it a quick glance and guessed it had been the mine manager's. The other door was locked.

From inside it came that rhythmic thumping. Now he could hear gasps and grunts. He tried the door. No use. He was ready to use a third bullet on it when he remembered the girl was most probably inside. He backed as far from the door as he could in the narrow hallway and poised himself to give a stiff-legged kick. The door opened. Dimly he sensed that something was wrong, that his body was not working the way it ought to. And somewhere he had a brand-new pain.

But inside the room were things to take his mind off pain at the moment. He stared, pistol in hand, and wondered if he dared laugh.

Miss Upton was bound to a kitchen chair, hands behind her. Red hair flying, Miss Upton was very much in action. She hadn't had much luck with her arms and hands but through constant effort she had managed slightly to loosen the bonds around her ankles until she could stand and even walk awkwardly, still bound in a crouching position to the chair. The chair legs were thin and round, their points tapered down to a half inch across. Miss Upton was raising herself and chair repeatedly, sitting down again with her full hundred pounds on the back legs of the chair. The back legs of the chair were punching tender spots in Ford's writhing body. The company bull's face was somewhat more puffy than usual, with a splinter from the Winchester stock protruding from his cheek just below his left eye. "You might save enough of him to hang," Wes ventured.

"Get me out of this goddamned chair!" Miss Upton suggested.

It was too much. For the first time in what he suspected must be over a year Wes found himself laughing uncontrollably. The girl must have been waiting for her chance. When he had attracted Ford's attention by blowing a Winchester out of his hands, the girl had backed into the company bull with those chair legs—from clear across the room. "Miss Upton," Wes said between gasps, "if you could cook I'd marry you."

"You've already sampled my cooking, Mr. Brooks," the girl said. "Now will you get me out of this chair?"

"Yes," Wes said, "I guess I will." He rummaged through his pockets and his knife was gone.

"Where did you ever get those trousers, Mr. Brooks?" Then abruptly she recognized the calf-length trousers and bottle-green shirt. "Oh!" There was a moment's silence. "Did you kill him?"

Wes shook his head. "He did," he said with a jab at the used-up company bull. "In front of all kinds of witnesses. Even if we don't manage to hang him for your father, he'll swing for shooting his accomplice."

There was a thump of shattering shingle and an instant later the sound of a shot. "How many friends's he got in town?" Wes asked.

Ford was beginning to realize he was no longer passing through Miss Upton's improvised stamp mill. He opened his eyes and groaned. "Who's shooting at us?" Wes asked him. Ford stared uncomprehendingly.

"If there's any danger of you gettin' away," Wes said, "it'll improve my disposition immeasurably to shoot you right now." He checked the Smith and Wesson. There were still four shots. Another bullet clipped a shingle from the roof. Wes aimed at the battered Ford and began squeezing the trigger on an empty cartridge.

Ford became more cooperative. "Ain't none of mine," he protested. "I don't know who's shootin'. Why don't you take a look at them crazy honyockers rode in with you?"

This same thought had just crossed Wes's mind.

"Come out with your hands up or we'll burn you out and the whole danged town with you!" It was a cracked old man's voice that Wes recognized. "Seems like it's my turn to burn down somebody else's house," Bridges added.

"Hold it," Wes yelled. "I got him dead to rights." Then under his breath he amended, "We got him."

He was still struggling with the knots that bound Miss Upton's hands when Bridges poked first his Hawken muzzle, then his own cautiously into the bedroom doorway. Wes was abruptly aware of how much nicer Miss Upton's abundant red hair smelled despite her recent ill usage. And he also realized that after the series of disasters that had befallen him he probably didn't smell much better than old man Bridges. "If you're thinkin' I need a bath, Miss Upton," he began.

"What I'm thinking, Mr. Brooks, is that although I enjoy your presence, if you don't go down to the kitchen soon and find a knife I may lose my restraint and make loud abusive noises."

Bridges grinned and produced a skinning knife from his greasy buckskins. A moment later the girl stood, rubbing her wrists. She was making instinctive womanly gestures at her hair when she finally noticed the extent of Wes's bloody contusions. They were downstairs in the kitchen when Tinacling appeared. "People are kind of edgy out there," he reported. "You want me to tell them anything?"

"Whatever you want," Wes said, adding an "Ouch" as Miss Upton's capable hands unbuttoned Polk's bottle-green shirt and exposed the crease along his ribs. "Ford do that?" she asked.

Wes nodded. Tinacling was driving the used-up company bull downstairs and out into the street. "Don't let them do it," Wes cautioned. "I want him to hang legal after he's straightened out who's who and where all the gold went."

The Indian boy changed his mind about displaying the prisoner. Turning him over to Bridges, he went back out to deliver some comforting words to the twittery townspeople of Opal.

"What on earth did you do to your leg, Mr. Brooks?"

Wes studied the shin he had skinned going through a stirrup, then saw she was looking at his bad knee, which was swollen until the loose pantsleg stretched. Then abruptly he knew what had felt wrong when he kicked in her bedroom door. He had done it *with his bad leg.* He moved his leg experimentally, winced and managed not to express an opinion. But the important thing was that his knee had moved, had actually bent. It had been the first time in over a year.

"Dunno," he said. "Hard tellin' if I'm gettin' worse or gettin' better." Then suddenly he was feeling much worse.

CHAPTER XXIII

When Wes awakened he had been cleaned up considerably, and for a moment he thought he was back in his boardinghouse room where Ford had shot Miss Upton's father. Then as his eyes focused, he saw he was in a strange room. Man's room, he supposed, unless ladies had gone to keeping razor strops hung from a bureau mirror brace. After another interval of dozing, he could guess who had last lived in this room.

He tried to move and the effort was so painful that he changed his mind. His chest was bandaged. His wrists were bandaged. His bad knee hung from a sling that dangled from a sapling framework over the bed. He wondered confusedly if this country had devised a new method of hanging. Then the girl came in.

Even bound to a chair, red hair flying in every direction, Miss Upton had exhibited no gross defects. Now she was considerably more attractive. As she sat beside him and began spooning soup into him Wes remembered he had once before lain in a hospital bed and endured a visit by a red-haired warrant officer's daughter. He was facing a critical moment in his life. "You uh—" He hesitated and tried again. "Have I been here long?"

"Only a few hours." She put more soup in his mouth.

When he had swallowed Wes asked, "Where's Ford?"

"Alive," the girl said. "The boy—the one you call Tina-cling—has been lecturing our citizens on the economics of mining gold and paying wages while losing profits. The citizens are agreed that Mr. Ford should not be lynched. Or at least that he should not be lynched before all the bank deposits in strange names have been traced and the Opal Mining and Development Company is sufficiently solvent to be able to increase wages." She spooned more soup into him and added, "Some townspeople also went down to Okapogum to see what the situation is there. There being no telephone to forewarn him, we may even catch Mr. Polk's brother and extract a confession."

"Wonder who the law is down there now that Hurley's dead."

"I'm sure we'll know within a day or two, Mr. Brooks. By the way, would it be proper for me to call you Wesley?"

"I'm afraid it wouldn't," Wes said. "I had a grandfather named Wesley. Trouble is, I also had one named Lester."

"Lesley?"

"Even worse."

"Could it be worse than Alberdeen?"

"You decide," Wes said. "It's Wester."

It was the first time Wes had ever seen Miss Upton laugh. He decided she looked even nicer laughing than she had struggling to get out of a chair.

Miss Upton controlled herself. "Tinacling and Mr. Bridges believe the bandits will soon be caught, too," she said. "There was some talk of shaming solid citizens into cleaning out the country's true troublemakers instead of burning down relatively inoffensive people's homes."

With a mob of Opal's citizenry accompanying them, Wes guessed it might turn out that way. If old Bridges were to show up alone, the Christians of Okapogum might decide the quickest way to assuage their consciences was to finish the old man off.

Four days passed and Tinacling returned with the news

that Ford and the surviving Polk brother shared a cell in the Okapogum pokey where they were dictating names, addresses, and bank account numbers to a lawyer, haggling mightily for their lives in return for putting the Opal Mining and Development Company back on its financial feet. The adjoining cell was occupied by some also-rans. These surviving bandits had also been found in possession of small amounts of gold for which their explanations were termed deficient.

"Bridges back in business again?" Wes asked.

"Not yet," the boy reported. "If he keeps on the way he's going now he may never work again."

"Oh?"

"Funny thing about all those Christians," the boy observed. "They may not be much for charity, but they're sure strong on guilt."

Wes and Miss Upton waited. They were in the parlor now, with Wes in a Morris chair, his still tender knee elevated on a footstool.

"Mr. Bridges is collecting for a building fund," the boy explained. "Doing quite well at it. Sometimes returns to the same house several times a day. He's gaining weight."

"If he don't watch out they're gonna trim his beard and change his clothes and civilize him to death." As he said this Wes noticed Miss Upton's speculative look.

Finally the boy was fed, had finished his news, and was leaving. "Where to?" Wes asked.

"My folks," Tinacling said. "Live about twenty miles up across the river."

"Any special reason?" Miss Upton asked.

"Well," Tinacling began hesitantly, "there's something we all have to do and I'm about the right age for it."

Wes decided it would be politic not to inquire about tribal ritual. "You'll be back?" he asked, and the boy assured them that he would. Wes made an inspired guess. "And when you come back you'll have a new name?" The boy gave him a surprised look and nodded.

He was gone and Wes and Miss Upton were alone in the house again. Wes was feeling enough better now to be acutely aware of his situation. He got to his feet and tried his new—old way of walking with two knees that both worked. For short distances he didn't need a cane. " 'Bout time I left too," he muttered.

"Where were you planning on going?" Miss Upton asked.

"No place special. Maybe now those bandits are in jail I can get a little peace back at my own place."

"Do you really aspire to be a farmer?"

"Wouldn't be a bad life I guess—if I knew something about it."

"You're a fast learner," Miss Upton said, "but now that the bandits are cleaned out, there are undoubtedly other men more fit to drive four-in-hand."

"Exactly."

"So what is there in life that you do well?"

"Ain't no way I'm goin' back in the army."

"You managed the affairs of soldiers. Can't you do the same for civilians?"

"You're pretty good at that yourself," Wes said. "Now that the snakes are all killed you won't have any trouble runnin' the mine."

"Possibly not," the girl said. "But there comes a time to look into one's soul and decide what things in life are important."

Wes was beginning to feel decidedly uncomfortable. "You don't want to run this mine?" he asked.

"I wanted to very much when my father was old and tired and needed help. Now . . ." She shrugged. "Now it's a means to an end. Now it's the welfare of a lot of people who depend on the mine's prosperity for their livelihood. Now it's other people's lives and other people's problems. I suppose you can't have one without the other."

"You'll make out," Wes said. "I never saw anybody less likely to make a failure of anything. Anyhow, you sure don't need me."

"Perhaps not. A young woman of property receives many offers. Do you find it unusual that she should be more interested in the one man who seems uninterested in acquiring wealth the easy way?"

"Ain't nobody works quite as hard for his money as the man who marries it."

"There will be plenty of work," the girl said. "What did she do to you?"

Wes stared. "What?"

"I'm twenty-five," the girl said. "You are at least ten years older than I."

"Twelve."

"It's been some time since you were a boy. Do you suppose I've spent my life wrapped in tinfoil just as you would have me think you have? What did she do to poison you?"

Abruptly Wes realized that this capable young lady with the abundant red hair was making a lot more sense than he was. "Nothing much really," he said. "She could read the future more accurately than I could. I s'pose that always makes a man nervous. Especially when a woman sees something he doesn't want to see."

It was Miss Upton's turn to sigh. "You disappoint me."

"Times when I disappoint myself," Wes admitted.

"I don't mean that," the girl snapped. "It takes a fool not to expect better of himself. What disappoints is that you expect less of me."

"I think you lost me there somewhere."

"I think I did not. Would you really be happier if I were to deceive you—conceal my intelligence, dedicate myself to convincing you every morning how wonderful you are?"

"Isn't that the way it's done? I'm not sayin' it's right but that's the way it is."

"Is it the money?"

"Partly."

"I can get rid of the mine—let the citizens of Opal manage their own affairs. Would you be happier scrabbling for a living in a tattered tent? Hunger and improper diet both seem to increase fertility. I'm sure our union would soon be blessed with children who would have been just as happy with a roof over their heads."

"You sure can make it sound attractive."

"Just what would you like?"

Wes thought a moment. "Well," he said, "we've had dinner already. Any chance of a cup of coffee, a shot of whiskey, and a cigar?"

Wordlessly the girl left the room. Wes sat alone with a sore but bendable knee. But it wasn't his knee that filled his thoughts. A half hour later he was still thinking, wondering what demon lurked within him that would not allow him to bend and accept the facts of life. Miss Upton was young. Miss Upton was very attractive. Miss Upton was smart. Miss Upton would soon be rich. Miss Upton wanted him. And no matter how he might manage to conceal it, Wes had been very aware of Miss Upton and her disruptive possibilities in the drear future that stretched before him. She was everything he might ask for—far more than he had ever dared hope for. And, like everything else in his life, he had bungled this chance too.

The house was empty. He got to his feet and limped about, practicing with bending both knees. A whistle blew for shift change and he guessed the sight of people was better than sitting here alone watching it grow dark. He limped through the doorway into the office, planning on grabbing a chair to sit out front in the fresh air. Then he saw the papers on the dead man's desk.

Upton's handwriting was hurried, but he had known what he was doing. Where his calculations left off and were taken up in a neat Spencerian hand things started going wrong. It was nothing glaring, but there were entries in the wrong column, credits magically converted into debits. Within another week the payroll would be in total chaos. He went back to the beginning of the ledger to make sure how Upton used to work it. The old man's methods were not all that different from the records any sergeant had to keep if he were to survive in the army. Wes considered erasing, knew there were too many errors, turned to a fresh page instead.

It turned dark and he stopped long enough to light a lamp. An hour passed and he ran over the page again. He was striking a trial balance when the door opened. Miss Upton came from the rear of the house with a tray. On it was a coffee pot and sidearms, a bottle of Old Crow, and a cigar.

"Thanks," Wes said, and went back to his figures. When he was satisfied he straightened and discovered his coffee was poured, creamed and sugared. The girl was nowhere in sight.

She was still not in sight when he had finished the coffee, had a single nip of Old Crow, and was on the short end of the cigar. His knee was reminding him that it was still not ready for prolonged sitting when he stubbed out the cigar and moved painfully through the darkened house and upstairs.

Morning came and he managed to shave himself with Upton's cutthroat razor. He went downstairs somewhat more easily than he had gone up last night. Miss Upton's good morning was grave. "Did you sleep well?" she added.

Wes assured her that he had. "Are you really that bad with figures?" he asked. "If you are you'd better find a good bookkeeper."

"Almost as bad as you are with horses," the girl confessed. "And when gold is involved, where does one find an honest bookkeeper?"

Wes had a sudden intuition. Where had Miss Upton been all the time between asking for a drink of whiskey and getting it? Any girl as coolly competent as this might also be able in half an hour to doctor up several pages of ledger.

Miss Upton was pouring coffee. He put his hand on her wrist until she put down the coffee pot and sat beside him. "Now tell me true, miss. Do you really not know the difference between a debit and a credit?"

Miss Upton gave a ghost of a smile. "Like you, I'm a quick learner, but nobody can know everything."

Wes knew there was still several things he didn't know about Miss Upton—might never know. But if he lived long enough it would be fun finding out.